# ONE OF A KIND

## KIND BROTHERS SERIES, BOOK 1

## SANDI LYNN

SANDI LYNN ROMANCE, LLC

# ONE OF A KIND

*New York Times, USA Today & Wall Street Journal* Bestselling
Author

Sandi Lynn

**One of a Kind**

Copyright © 2021 Sandi Lynn Romance, LLC

Photo by Wander Aguiar
Model: Sam M.

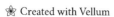 Created with Vellum

# MISSION STATEMENT

Sandi Lynn Romance

Providing readers with romance novels that will whisk
them away
to another world and from the daily grind of life – one book
at a time.

# CHAPTER 1

*S*am
      I opened my eyes, and with the slight turn of my head, I cringed when I saw her lying there.

"Shit," I whispered to myself as I brought my arm up and laid it across my forehead.

"Good morning." A bright smile crossed her lips as her finger slid down my bare chest.

"Morning."

I climbed out of bed, went into the bathroom, and shut the door. Gripping the edge of the sink, I leaned forward and lowered my head for a moment before looking in the mirror and asking myself what the fuck I'd done. My head was pounding from all the alcohol I drank last night at our birthday bash. Did I regret it? No. The only thing I regretted was sleeping with Kendra.

My brothers, Stefan, Sebastian, Simon, and I rented out the Rhythm Room in L.A., where a hundred of our friends and office staff attended to celebrate our thirty-second birthday. We all drank too much, and I didn't remember getting home, nor did I remember Kendra accompanying me. Shit.

Walking back out to the bedroom, Kendra lay there and scrolled on her phone.

"Kendra, we need—"

"Come back to bed." A smile overtook her face as she held the sheet up.

"I can't right now." I walked over to my pants lying on the floor, pulled my phone from my pocket, and sent a text message to my brothers.

*"Need to surf. Anybody up for it? I'm heading out there in a few."*

I looked up from my phone and over at Kendra, who was still in my bed.

"Listen, Kendra," I said as I walked over to her. "Last night shouldn't have happened, and I'm sorry. I was really drunk, and I crossed the line. It will never happen again, and I just want to make that very clear."

"But Sam—" She brought her hand up to my cheek as tears filled her eyes.

"No buts, Kendra. It was a mistake, and I'm sorry."

"Okay." Her voice whispered as she slowly nodded her head.

I stood up from the edge of the bed, grabbed her clothes from the floor, and handed them to her. Walking over to the dresser, I pulled a pair of board shorts out of the drawer and slipped them on.

"I'm heading out. I'll see you on Monday."

I stepped out the sliding door off the kitchen, grabbed my surfboard from the deck, and headed down to the beach.

"Why, Sam?" I heard my brother Stefan shout as he walked towards me. "I'm so hungover right now."

"So am I. But once we hit the cold water, we'll feel better. You know that."

Looking over Stefan's shoulder, I saw Simon and Sebastian heading towards us.

"Are we going to do this or what?" Sebastian said as he ran by us and put his board in the water.

The four of us paddled out, and I had to tell them about Kendra. They were my brothers, and we told each other everything.

"I slept with Kendra last night."

"What?!" Stefan exclaimed. "Come on, Sam. Not again."

"I honestly don't remember anything. I was just as surprised as you when I woke up and saw her lying there."

"Isn't she like the fourth assistant you've slept with?" Simon smirked.

"Shut up." I splashed him.

"She's going to quit," Stefan said. "And then we're going to have to hire someone else. She's only been there three months, bro."

"She's a mature woman. She'll be okay."

"Women are not okay after sleeping with you," Sebastian said.

"Like any of you can talk. You're no strangers at leaving a trail of broken hearts."

"True. But at least we don't work in the same office with the women we sleep with." Simon smirked.

My brothers and I were quadruplets who were conceived naturally when our parents were twenty-two years old. They said ninety percent of quadruplets conceived are done through fertility treatments and IVF. We were the natural ten percent. The second we were born, our mother had her tubes tied. Four children all at once were enough for her, our father, and their marriage. Unfortunately, the stress of raising the four of us at the same time was too much of a strain on their marriage. My father was just starting his architectural firm and was barely ever home to help. His work consumed him, and he used the excuse of having to put in the time and effort to make sure the company made enough money to provide for us. They ended up divorcing when we were just five years old. I remembered the fights, the screaming, the arguing, and the tears that fell down my mother's face more times than not. In the custody battle, my father was awarded joint custody of us, and we traveled back and forth between homes. Since that time, my mother married a man named Jacob. They were together ten years before he cheated on her, and she divorced him. Then she met her current husband, Curtis, and they've been together since. As for my father, he'd been married and divorced four times and was now getting married for a fifth time to a woman named Celeste.

My brothers and I had never seen a healthy relationship. We'd only saw the destruction and chaos it caused. It was enough to turn us off from having any type of relationship with women, except a sexual one. We'd made a pact. One that would keep us single and living the bachelor life with no strings and no drama. Except for my brother, Stefan. He ended up getting a girl named Monica pregnant when he was twenty-three years old. When Lily turned three, Monica dropped her off at Stefan's house for his weekend visit and never came back. That was five years ago. Now, he was a single father to an eight-year-old girl whom we loved very much and would do anything to protect her.

~

We finished our surfing and headed back to our homes. A few years ago, our father bought a stretch of property along the beach in Venice. He was going to build high-rise condos but instead gave it to us to build our own homes. I designed them, and Stefan built them. We both worked at Kind Design & Architecture. The company, my father, started when we were babies and grew to be one of the largest architectural firms in the country. I ran the architect division, and Stefan ran the building division. As for my other two brothers, they had other interests. Sebastian loved to cook and owns his own five Michelin star restaurant in Los Angeles, and Simon became a homicide detective for the LAPD.

I said goodbye to my brothers and stepped inside my luxury beach house, praying that Kendra had left. When I walked into the bedroom, I saw the bed was made, and she was gone. Monday was going to be uncomfortable, to say the least. I couldn't help that I always hired beautiful women, and I couldn't help that I couldn't keep my dick in my pants. I'd done good keeping away from Kendra the past three months, even though she tempted me on more than one occasion. Maybe I needed not to drink so much in the presence of beautiful women.

# CHAPTER 2

## TWO WEEKS LATER

*S*am

Things with Kendra were out of control. She started to come to work in very provocative clothing. More so than before. Her blouses were unbuttoned a little further, her skirts were shorter, and her heels were higher. One day, she walked in wearing a sheer blouse without a bra. When I told her that was inappropriate for the office, she said she figured I'd like it and found it sexy. It was, don't get me wrong, but it was still inappropriate.

I was sitting at my desk when Grayson, our human resources manager, came to my office.

"You got a minute, Sam?"

"Sure, Grayson. Have a seat."

"Kendra was just in my office."

"Really?" I cocked my head and furrowed my brows. "She called in sick today."

"She quit, and she said it was because you created a hostile work environment, and she couldn't deal with the pressure anymore. It wasn't good for her mental health."

"I did not create a hostile work environment. What the hell is she talking about?"

"She said you criticized her clothing, you constantly yelled at her, and you made her feel worthless and unworthy as your personal assistant. You slept with her, didn't you?"

"First of all, she's lying. She came to work in a sheer blouse with no bra on. Her tits were as visible as the sun on a clear day. I told her it was inappropriate, and I sent her home to change. And yes, I slept with her. But I didn't know I did until the next morning. It happened the night of the birthday party. I had way too much to drink."

"Do I need to tell your father about this?" His brow arched.

"No. You do not." I pointed at him. "If he asks, just tell him she found a better job or something."

"All right." He let out a sigh. "Now, I need to start looking for another assistant for you."

"Do me a favor, and I'm very serious, Grayson. Make sure she's not attractive at all, and she's a lot older. Maybe a woman in her fifties or something."

"Why? You'd still sleep with a woman in her forties?"

"If she was sexy as hell, yes." I smirked. "Find me someone like Joan."

"And you think someone in their fifties is going to put up with your shit? The only reason Joan does is because she's known you since you were a kid."

"Just make sure the woman you hire isn't attractive so that I won't be tempted."

He got up from his seat and shook his head all the way out of my office. Picking up the phone, I dialed Stefan.

"What's up, bro?"

"Come to my office."

"On my way. What's up?" he asked as he stepped inside.

"Kendra quit."

"Shocker!" He shook his head.

"She told Grayson I created a hostile work environment, and I made her feel unworthy and worthless as my assistant."

"You know I never cared for her. Something always seemed off. And she was always in a bad mood. Honestly, I'm glad she quit. So now what?"

"Grayson is going to find me an unattractive and older assistant. One that I won't be tempted to bend over my desk and fuck every day."

"Good." He pointed at me. "That's exactly what you need. I have to run. I'm picking Lily up from school today."

"Where's Nanny Kate?"

"She has jury duty today. I'll talk to you later. Good job on losing another personal assistant. I knew you could do it." His lips gave way to a smirk as he walked out of my office.

I let out a long sigh as I leaned back in my chair.

"Joan, can you come in here, please?" I asked over the intercom.

"What can I do for you, Sam?"

"I want you to know that Kendra quit."

"Thank the lord." She made the sign of the cross. "I never liked that floozy of a girl."

"I know you didn't."

"She was rude, always in a bad mood, and chewed her gum like an ape. Not to mention her choice of clothing was —" She put her hand up and shook her head.

I couldn't help but let out a laugh.

"Grayson is working on finding me another personal assistant."

"Can you do me a favor and not sleep with this one? I'm getting a little tired of training these women."

"I already told Grayson to make sure she's not attractive and a lot older."

"No one older than their mid-thirties will put up with your crap."

"Why does everyone keep saying that?" My brows furrowed.

# CHAPTER 3

*J*ulia

I had just walked through the door when my phone rang. Pulling it from my purse, I saw Mrs. Hart was calling. Suddenly, a sick feeling rose inside me.

"Hello."

"Julia, Steven is asking for you."

"I'm on my way."

I climbed in my car and headed straight to Steven's house. When I arrived, Gina, his wife, greeted me in the foyer.

"Thank you for coming over so late."

"Oh my gosh. It's totally fine. You know I would do anything for him."

"I know." A weary smile crossed her face. "He's declined since you were here two days ago. I just want you to be prepared."

"Thanks, Gina."

I went to the bedroom, and the moment I stepped through the door, he turned his head and looked at me.

"Thanks for coming, sweetheart."

"Of course." I walked over and took hold of his hand.

"Did you deliver those contracts?"

"I did. And I sent the emails you asked me to and picked up the bracelet you ordered for Gina. It's all gift wrapped and ready to give to her."

"Thank you, my dear."

I stayed and talked with him for a while until he fell asleep. After quietly walking out of the room, I went into the kitchen, where Gina was sitting at the table drinking a glass of wine.

"Would you like a glass of wine?"

"No. Thank you. He's asleep now, so I'm going to head home."

"Okay." She stood up and gave me a hug. "Thanks for coming by. I know it meant a lot to him."

"Of course. Are you okay?"

"I'm hanging in there."

"If there's anything you need, call me."

"Thank you, Julia."

I gave her a hug goodbye and headed home.

∾

### One Week Later

*a*s I walked by Steven's casket, I laid down a single red rose on top of it. It was hard to believe he was gone. One minute he was healthy, and the next, he was given a few months to live. As I was on my way to the funeral luncheon, my phone rang with an unfamiliar number.

"Hello."

"Hi. Is this Julia Benton?" A man's voice on the other end asked.

"Yes."

"Ms. Benton, my name is Grayson Peterson, and I'm the

human resources director at Kind Design and Architecture in downtown Los Angeles. I received your resume and a recommendation letter from Mr. Steven Hart."

"You did?"

"Yes. I'm currently interviewing candidates for the personal assistant position we have available, and you came highly recommended. I would like you to come in for an interview if you're interested."

I was caught off guard and took a moment to process what Mr. Peterson had just said.

"Hello? Ms. Benton, are you still there?"

"Yes. I'm sorry. Can you tell me when you received my resume and recommendation letter?"

"I received it five days ago. I'm sorry I didn't reach out sooner, but I was out of town. Mr. Hart said you would be needing a job, and he couldn't recommend you enough. Would you be interested in coming in for an interview?"

"Sure. I guess."

"Great. How is tomorrow morning at ten a.m.?"

"That's good. Can you text me your address?"

"Of course. I'll send it when we hang up. I look forward to meeting you."

"Thank you, Mr. Peterson."

When I pulled up to the Hart home, I climbed out of my car and stepped inside, where I found Gina in the living room staring at the portrait of her and Steven that hung above the fireplace. I made my way through the crowd of people who were talking, drinking, and eating the catered food Gina had arranged. Walking over to her, I placed my hand on her arm, and she turned her head while a small smile graced her face.

"Thanks for coming, Julia."

"You know I would never miss this. Can I talk to you for a moment?"

"Of course." I followed her into the library.

"On my way over, I got a call from Grayson Peterson from Kind Design & Architecture wanting me to come in for an interview for a personal assistant position."

"I was going to tell you about that, but with everything going on, it slipped my mind. Steven had me send your resume and the recommendation letter over to them the morning after you visited him."

"Why would he do that?"

"You know Steven, Julia. He always had to have all his ducks in a row." A smile crossed her lips. "Including his funeral. Right down to the last detail. He didn't want you to worry about a job. You know he loved you, and we always considered you a part of this family. He was just looking out for you the way you always looked out for him." She took hold of my hand and gave it a gentle squeeze.

# CHAPTER 4

*J*ulia

Traffic wasn't as bad today for some strange reason, which had me arriving thirty minutes early for my interview. I had one of two choices. I could sit in my car and aimlessly scroll through Facebook or Instagram, or I could walk across the street to the Starlight café and grab a coffee and pastry.

I climbed out of my car and headed across the street. When I stepped inside the café, I stood in the short line and patiently waited my turn.

"Hi there. How can I help you?" The cute guy behind the counter smiled brightly.

"Hi. Good morning." I grinned. "I'll have a medium hazelnut coffee. Also, I'll take that apple turnover." I pointed to the case.

"Coming right up."

"Excuse me." A deep voice came from behind. "Do you have any more of those apple turnovers?"

"No. I'm sorry. That's the last one."

"It's only nine-thirty in the morning. How is it the last one already?"

Turning around, I gasped when my eyes locked on the man with irritation in his voice.

"It's yours." I gave him a wide smile.

"Excuse me?" His bright blue eyes stared into mine.

"The apple turnover. You can have it."

"It's fine. I'll get something else."

"Nope. I insist. I don't need the sugar or the carbs anyway. I'm really not sure why I even ordered it." I cocked my head.

"Well, it looks to me like you could use a few carbs."

"Thanks — I think." My brows furrowed. "Anyway, take the turnover."

"Thank you. Let me buy your coffee then for being so kind."

"You don't have to do that."

"I know I don't have to. I want to. As a thank you for surrendering your turnover."

"If you insist." The corners of my mouth curved upward.

"Here's your coffee, miss. I hope you have a good day!"

"Thank you. You, too."

I turned and looked at the dreamy man in the expensive suit who stood six foot two with broad shoulders, short dark hair, a well-trimmed five o'clock shadow, and the bluest eyes I'd ever seen. Damn. Just damn. My heart wouldn't stop racing.

"Enjoy your turnover and your day." I grinned before walking out of the café.

"Same to you."

When I stepped outside the café, I let out a deep breath. He was one hell of a sexy man. I had to stop for a moment and think if I'd ever seen a man so handsome in my life. I had, and he was the second one in my lifetime.

Looking at my watch, it was nine fifty. I took a few more

sips of my coffee and threw it in the trash can outside the building.

~

"Miss Benton, Mr. Peterson will see you now. Follow me." The tall, slender woman with auburn-colored hair smiled as she led me down the hallway.

When she opened the door to Mr. Peterson's office, the look on his face when he saw me struck me as strange.

"You must be Julia. I'm Grayson." He extended his hand.

"It's nice to meet you, Grayson."

"Please, have a seat." He gestured to the black chair across from his desk. "So, tell me why you left your position at Hart Industries."

"Mr. Hart passed away last week."

"I'm sorry. I had no idea he'd passed away. I see you worked for him for the past three and a half years, and prior to that, you were an assistant manager at a coffee shop."

"Yes."

"The letter he sent along with your resume was very enduring. He must have really liked you."

"He and his wife, Gina, considered me part of their family."

"In his letter, he stated that you were extremely flexible, trustworthy, have excellent communication skills, organized and proactive. He also goes on to say that you are a master at multitasking, you're very smart, and a hard worker. In all honesty, Julia, Steven Hart makes you out to be a godsend of an employee."

"I take pride in my work, Grayson."

He leaned back in his chair and stared at me for a moment. Something told me he was hesitant about what he was going to say next.

"You are by far the best candidate I've interviewed. If you came to work for us, you'd be the personal assistant to Mr. Sam Kind, the president of the company and architect division."

"May I ask why his other personal assistant is no longer working for him?"

He inhaled a sharp breath and shifted nervously in his chair.

"Well…there were some personality conflicts."

"I see. Is he a difficult man to work for?"

"Not really. The person who works for him will need a strong personality. Kendra, his last personal assistant, didn't have one."

"So, he is a difficult man?" I cocked my head. "It doesn't matter. I can handle anybody and work with anyone, even under strenuous situations. I don't let people get to me, Grayson. No matter their personality because there's always some deep-rooted issue behind the scenes in their personal life."

"Wow. I really like you, Julia. Here is the pay structure and the benefits package." He handed me a folder.

Opening it, I looked over the paperwork inside.

"This looks good. What about raises?"

"At the end of ninety days, you'll be issued a review, and if all the boxes are checked, and you're exceeding expectations, you'll get a raise and a bonus. I'd like to offer you the position if you're interested."

"Well, I do need a job. So yes, I would love to work for Kind Design & Architecture." A bright smile crossed my face.

"Excellent! Can you start first thing Monday morning?"

"I'll see you then." I smiled as I stood up from my chair and extended my hand.

# CHAPTER 5

*S*am

"Is that an apple turnover from across the street?" Stefan asked as he stepped into my office.

"It is." I broke off a piece and handed it to him.

"Thanks, bro."

"I almost didn't get it," I said before taking a sip of my coffee.

"What do you mean?"

"There was this woman in front of me, and she took the last one. When she heard me ask if there were anymore and there weren't, she let me have it."

"Why? Did you hypnotize her with your dreamy blue eyes?" He smirked.

"Shut up. She just told me to take it. I don't know. She was nice. Like, really nice." My brows furrowed. "But being nice wasn't the only thing about her."

"Do tell, brother."

I let out a sigh as I leaned back in my chair.

"She was stunningly beautiful."

"And? What did she look like?"

"She was about 5'6, maybe 5'7. She had long dark wavy hair, and her eyes," I paused, "they were like a smoky blue but more of a gray if that makes sense. I'd never seen eyes like that before. She was just sexy as hell. Especially in the tailored pantsuit, she was wearing. Damn. What I wouldn't give to see what she was hiding underneath. My imagination really went into overdrive."

"Did you get her number so you could properly thank her for giving you the last apple turnover?"

"Nah. I paid for her coffee."

"What?" He laughed. "Why didn't you ask her out or for her number?"

"I don't know. It all happened so fast. Plus, there was this innocence about her. I can't explain it."

"Well, you blew your chance, bro. Anyway, I'm heading out. I have to pick up Lily. She has a half-day of school today."

"Nanny Kate still has jury duty?"

"Yeah. She got picked for a case. I'll talk to you later."

While I was sitting at my drafting table putting the final touches on a building design, my phone rang. When I looked over at it, I saw Sebastian was calling.

"Talk to me," I answered.

"Do you have plans for tonight?"

"Not as of right now. Why?"

"There's a new bar that just opened up on West 6th Street. Simon and I are both off tonight, and we're going to check it out. Come with us."

"Sounds good. I'm in."

"Great. I already talked to Stefan, and he's in too."

"What time?"

"We were thinking around seven-thirty. Just meet at my house, and we'll all drive together."

"Sounds good. I'll see you then."

Just as I ended the call, Grayson walked into my office.

"Hey, Sam. Do you have a second?"

"Sure. What's up?" I turned my chair around and looked at him.

"Your new personal assistant starts Monday morning."

"Great. Tell me about her."

"Her skills are impeccable, and she came highly recommended by her previous employer. She was by far the best candidate for the job."

"And?" I narrowed my eye at him.

"And what?"

"Age, looks, etc."

"She's twenty-eight—"

"Oh, come on, Grayson." I interrupted him mid-sentence.

He put his hand up. "Just listen to me. She's not your type at all. In fact, she's a very mousy-looking girl. Very plain. Totally not your type. But she has everything else you're looking for in a personal assistant."

"Okay. I trust you."

"What's her name?"

Suddenly his phone rang, and when he looked at it, he quickly answered.

"We'll talk later," he mouthed before walking out of my office.

~

*M*y brothers and I arrived at Untapped. A new bar that had just opened a couple of days ago. The place was packed, and we were lucky enough to get the only table available.

"Damn. Look at this place," Simon said.

"Hey, boys." The cute blonde waitress flirted. "What can I get you?"

"I'll have a single malt scotch, 17 years," I spoke.

"I'll have a bourbon," Stefan said.

"I'll have a single malt scotch as well," Sebastian spoke.

"17 years?" The waitress asked.

"Yeah. That's fine."

"And for you?" she asked Simon.

"I'll have a crown royal."

"Coming right up. There are menus right there if you want to place a food order. I'll be back with your drinks."

A few moments later, the waitress walked over with our drinks and took our food order. Sitting at the table across from us were four women who wouldn't stop staring as they whispered to each other. We were used to it. It happened every time we went out together.

"We still need to go get our tuxes for the wedding," Sebastian spoke. "We should all just set a time and meet there."

"You know, I'm getting a little tired of standing up in Dad's weddings," I spoke.

"No shit." Simon shook his head as he picked up his drink.

"I need another scotch. Where is our waitress?" I spoke with irritation.

"It's busy. She probably can't keep up," Sebastian said.

"I'll go up to the bar and get the drinks myself. Refills?" I looked at my brothers.

I was heading up to the bar when my eyes caught sight of the beautiful woman from this morning sitting on one of the stools with a drink in her hand.

# CHAPTER 6

*J*ulia

Pulling my phone from my purse to check the time, I saw I had a text message from my friend, Mandy.

*"You're never going to believe it. My car broke down on the expressway. I called Todd, and he's on his way to get me. I'm sorry, Julia, but I won't be able to make it."*

*"Are you okay?"*

*"I'm fine. I told Todd we're going to the dealership first thing tomorrow morning and buying me a new one. This is the third time it broke down this month. I'm sorry. I know you're waiting for me."*

*"It's okay. Things happen. Don't give it another thought. It's a great bar, and we'll come check it out together next week. I'm just going to have one more drink and head home. You be safe."*

*"I will, my friend. You, too. Don't be talking to any strange guys."*

*"Who me?"* I sent her the wink emoji.

Suddenly, I heard this voice next to me.

"Twice in one day. It must be fate."

Looking up from my phone, the corners of my mouth

curved upward when I saw the handsome man from this morning.

"I bet you say that to all the women."

"Only the ones I find incredibly attractive." A sexy grin graced his face.

"Can I buy you another drink?" he asked as he looked at my empty glass.

"You already bought my coffee this morning."

"Is there a rule or a law that says I can't buy you another beverage in the same day?"

"I don't think so." I laughed.

"Is that a martini?"

"A lemon martini."

"Bartender, another lemon martini for the lady," he spoke. "And a single malt scotch, 17 years, for me."

"Coming right up."

"Please tell me you're not here by yourself, or worse yet, with a man." He smirked.

"I was supposed to meet my friend, but she is currently broken down on the expressway."

"She broke down, or her car broke down?"

"Her car." I couldn't help but laugh, and the smile on his face widened.

"I'm Sam." He extended his hand.

"Julia." I placed my hand in his.

"It's nice to meet you, Julia."

"Sam, what's taking you so long? We're getting thirsty over there," a handsome man asked as he walked over.

"Stefan, this is Julia. Julia, my brother, Stefan."

*Good God. There were two of them.*

"Hi, Stefan." I extended my hand. "It's nice to meet you."

"The pleasure is all mine." He smiled as he shook my hand.

"If you don't mind, Stefan." Sam shot him a look.

"I'll just flag down our waitress." He turned and walked away.

"Sorry about that," Sam said.

"It's totally fine. Do you have any other siblings?"

"I do. I have two more brothers, and they're sitting at that table right over there." He pointed.

Turning my head, it wasn't hard to miss the table with the three sexy as sin men sitting at it.

"Those are your brothers?"

"Yes."

"You all look the same age."

"That's because we are. We just turned thirty-two a few days ago."

"You're quadruplets?" My brows raised in shock.

"We are."

"Wow. I have a twin sister, but I've never met quadruplets before. Who's the oldest?"

"I am. Stefan was born two minutes after me. Then Sebastian was born two minutes after him, and then there was Simon who took a little longer by four minutes."

"That is really amazing." I grinned. "Your mom must have had her hands full with four little boys running around."

"She did." His lips gave way to a smirk.

"Here's the fried mushrooms you ordered. Sorry, it took so long," the bartender spoke as he set the plate down in front of me.

"That's okay. I know you're busy." I gave him a smile. "Fried mushroom?" I asked Sam.

"Sure." He smiled as he took one. "Be careful. They're hot."

"Trust me. I know. I've burnt my mouth one too many times on these."

After I ate a couple, Sam lightly ran his thumb down the side of my mouth.

"You had a crumb there."

I swallowed hard because this man was way too sexy, and the only thing going through my mind while we talked was his naked body on top of mine or from behind.

"Thank you." My eyes stayed locked on his.

"You're welcome." The corners of his mouth curved up into a sexy grin that sent shivers down my spine.

This was the moment. The moment where I knew sex with him was inevitable. I didn't know this man from Adam, but his extreme Adonis looks, confidence, and masculinity captivated me and sent my ovaries into overdrive. I'd had plenty of one-night stands the past four years. It was a way for me to enjoy the pleasure of a man when I needed it without any attachment. But I was always careful whom I chose to have a one-night stand with. I'd never had one when I was completely inebriated because to me, that qualified as the walk of shame. I wasn't in control. But if I chose the man and he fulfilled the desire inside me, I considered it a victory lap. And somehow, I knew Sam would fulfill every desire I wanted and needed right at this moment.

"Have I told you how stunning you are?"

"Why is that? Because I let you have the last apple turnover this morning." My lips gave way to a smirk.

"Well, that was just a bonus." He finished his scotch. "You're a beautiful and sexy woman."

"Looks like our glasses are empty. We could go back to my place and have a nightcap." I ran my finger across his hand that was resting on the bar.

"I don't have a car here. I rode with my brothers."

"In that case, I can give you a ride home."

"Let's go." He smiled as he pulled some cash from his wallet and threw it down. "I just need to go tell my brothers I'm leaving. I'll meet you out front?"

"I'll meet you out front," I said as I grabbed my purse.

*~*

*S*am

I kept my hand in my pocket to keep my cock under control while I walked back to the table.

"If you don't mind, I'm leaving, and Julia is going to drive me home."

"She's hot, bro. Good job." Sebastian smiled.

"Good for you, Sam," my brother Simon spoke.

"Wait before you go. She looks like the woman you described to me earlier. The one from the café this morning."

"That is her. Can you believe it?" I smiled and then turned and headed towards the door.

"My car is down here," Julia said as we walked down the street.

When we approached her white Jeep Sahara, she threw the keys at me.

"You drive. It'll be easier than you giving me directions the whole way there." She grinned.

"Okay." I smiled at her as we climbed into the car.

"By the way, where do you live?"

"Venice."

"Nice. With your brothers?"

"No." He let out a chuckle. "I live alone, but my brothers are my neighbors. We live in our own homes right next to each other on the beach."

"Wow. Really?" She cocked her head.

"Yeah." I turned my head and smiled at her. "Is that hard to believe?"

"No. Not really, considering I live with my sister."

"And where is that?"

"Downtown. In the Circa building."

"Nice. Those are great apartments."

"Yeah. I like it there. My sister left for Europe a few weeks ago, and she'll be gone for another month."

"For work or pleasure?" I asked.

"Work. She's a fashion model, and she's doing a few campaign shoots."

"A model? Really? Are you two identical?"

"No. We're fraternal."

"You didn't want to get into the modeling business?"

"Nah. That isn't my scene."

"What is your scene?" I asked as I glanced over at her.

"Coffee and cozy coffee shops. I'm going to own one, one day."

"A coffee shop? Really?"

"Yeah. It's always been a dream of mine."

# CHAPTER 7

*J*ulia

Before I could ask him what he did for a living, we pulled into his driveway, and I was enthralled by the modern-looking and sophisticated Hampton-style home.

"Wow. I love this," I said as I climbed out of my jeep.

"Thanks. My brother Sebastian lives on this side," he pointed to the right. "Stefan lives to my left, and Simon's house is next to Stefan's."

We stepped into the house through the side door next to the garage, which led into the kitchen. A big and elegant gourmet kitchen with a breakfast nook and the most incredible view of the ocean.

Sam threw his keys down on the counter, walked over to me, and placed his hands on my hips.

"Can I get you something to drink?"

"No. I'm good." I wrapped my arms around him.

Suddenly, he leaned in and smashed his lips against the flesh of my neck. Goosebumps soared over my body as the burning desire down below intensified. His lips met mine, and instantly our tongues collided. My heart was pounding out of my chest with excitement as he took down the straps of my dress, unzipped the back, and let it fall to the ground. His hands groped my bare breasts, and his fingers plucked at my hardened peaks.

"You are so goddamn beautiful."

His hand moved down my torso, and his fingers slipped down the front of my panties. I gasped at the feel when he dipped his finger inside. I'd quickly undone his belt and his pants and stuck my hand down the front of them and grabbed a hold of his thick hard cock while he explored me. Nothing gave me greater pleasure than knowing the treat I was in for. It felt like Christmas day, and I was more than ready for my gift. He pushed me up against the wall in the living room and placed one hand against the wall while the other was exploring me down below. His hard and muscular body pressed against me as our lips tangled. My moans heightened, and my heart raced as an orgasm flowed through me.

"I'm not done with you yet," he spoke. "I need to taste what I've been dying to since the moment I met you."

He got on his knees and pressed his mouth against my most sensitive area, stroking my clit with his tongue while I moaned, and my fingers tangled in his hair. Standing up, he took down his pants, and I saw first-hand what my hand had felt. The gods had truly blessed him, and I silently thanked them. Ripping the corner of the wrapper, he rolled the condom over his cock, lifted me up, and held me with his strong arms as he thrust inside me. Our lips met again as he moved swiftly in and out. My body trembled with pleasure as my legs were wrapped tightly around his waist, locking him against me.

He carried me up to his bedroom as he was buried inside me. Laying me on the bed, he moved in and out while his mouth explored my breasts. I was swelling with delight and on the verge of another orgasm. What was happening? I'd never had two orgasms with a one-night stand before. His skills were beyond mad, and my body had no choice but to succumb to him. My nails dug into the flesh of his back as I let out several moans while I rode the pleasure wave. His movement became faster as beads of sweat formed on his forehead. The sounds that emerged from him were sexy as hell, and he halted and exploded inside me. His body dropped onto mine, and I slowly stroked his back while we waited for our breathing rate to slow down. Lifting his head, he looked at me.

"Are you okay?" he asked in a soft voice.

"I'm more than okay. You?"

"Same." He smiled as he kissed my lips and climbed off me. "You can stay the night if you want. It's late for you to be driving home," he said as he went into the bathroom.

"Sure. I think I will. I'm really tired." I let out a yawn.

"I'm heading out early. Every Saturday morning, my brothers and I go surfing."

"Okay. Just wake me if I'm not up."

"I will. Good night, Julia."

"Good night, Sam." I gave him a smile as I rolled over.

The next morning, I opened my eyes, and Sam wasn't in bed. Looking at the clock, it was six-thirty a.m. I let out a long yawn and noticed my dress was hanging on a hanger on the door. He must have brought it up from downstairs along with my panties that were sitting on his dresser. Climbing out of bed, I slipped into them and went downstairs.

"Good morning. I was just coming to wake you," he said as I stepped into the kitchen.

"Good morning."

"I made you a cup of coffee before you head out. Do you take cream or sugar?"

"Just black."

"Really?" His brow arched. "How do you do that? I need to add cream to mine." He handed me a cup.

"Coffee is a delicacy. Like a fine wine. If you overload it with creams and sugars, you're taking away from the unique taste, aroma, and notes of the different flavorings of the beans."

"Uh-huh." He slowly nodded his head as he held the creamer over his cup. "So, you're telling me you never drink any types of lattes, macchiatos, etc.? You just drink plain black coffee all the time?"

"No. I love me a good latte or macchiato every now and again. I'm just saying if you're having a regular cup of coffee, it should be black and not smothered with cream or sugar."

He took a spoon from the drawer, stirred his coffee, and held up his cup.

"This is my latte." He gave me a wink as a smirk crossed his lips. "Listen, Julia, before you go, we should talk about something."

"Sure." I took a sip of my coffee.

"Last night was great. It was amazing, but I'm not going to ask you for your phone number or ask you on a date. This was just a one-time thing."

"Yeah. I know." I nodded my head.

"You do?"

"Yeah. It was just a one-time thing for me too. I wasn't expecting you to call me."

"You weren't?" His brows furrowed.

"No. We were attracted to each other last night, had some fun, and now it's time to part ways." I set my coffee cup down on the counter. "Thanks for the hook-up last night, but I must go. Do you know where my shoes are?" I looked around.

"I put them by the front door." The frown never left his face.

Walking over to him, I extended my hand.

"It was nice to meet you, Sam."

"It was nice to meet you too, Julia." He lightly shook my hand.

"Maybe we'll run into each other again someday. Enjoy surfing with your brothers." I smiled as I headed towards the door.

"Uh, yeah. Have a good weekend."

I slipped into my shoes, grabbed my purse, and walked out.

# CHAPTER 8

*S*am
    I grabbed my surfboard and headed down to the water, where my brothers were waiting for me.

"Well, how did it go last night?" Simon asked.

"It was great."

"And this morning when you kicked her out?" Stefan asked.

"I really didn't have to. She couldn't get out fast enough."

"What?" Sebastian laughed. "What do you mean?"

"After she lectured me about how I shouldn't put cream in my coffee, I told her this was a one-time thing, and I wasn't going to ask for her number or ask her out. She told me last night was a one-time thing for her too, and then she thanked me for the hook-up, put on her shoes, and left. In fact, she was really happy. It was weird."

"That is weird," Simon said as we put our boards in the water and climbed on.

"Bro, she could be one of those women who act like it's okay, and then she's going to stalk your ass. It wouldn't be the first time," Stefan spoke. "Mom and I are taking Lily to Pacific Park today. You guys want to tag along?"

"Nah. I'm working," Sebastian said.

"I'm going to head to the office after and do some work," I spoke.

"I'm meeting up with Chris later, and we're going golfing."

"Ha. Have fun with Mom." I grinned as I saw a wave coming.

Later that night, I was getting ready to head out to meet my friend, Benny, for dinner. As I walked out of the bathroom and looked at the bed, thoughts about Julia flowed through my mind. In fact, I hadn't stopped thinking about her all day. Even when I was at work, I kept getting distracted by thoughts of her and last night. Sighing, I put on my watch, grabbed my wallet from the dresser, and headed out for the night.

~

I got into the office early to start on a new design before my new assistant arrived. Thank God she was starting today. I wasn't sure how much longer I could have gone without one. My mind was in a good space, and I knew this one was going to work out. Not only did Grayson say she had impeccable skills, but he assured me she wasn't my type at all, which was good. No temptation, no losing a personal assistant.

I was sitting at my drafting table sketching when there was a knock on the door. When it opened, I heard Grayson's voice.

"Sam, I'd like you to meet your new personal—"

Turning around, my eyes widened when I saw who was standing next to him.

"Julia?"

"Sam? Well, this is awkward." She grinned.

"Hold on a second," Grayson's voice raised. "You two know each other?"

"We met briefly the other night," Julia spoke.

I gave Grayson a stern look, for he lied to me.

"Great." He shook his head. "Just great." He turned and walked out of my office.

"Hi again." She smiled and gave me a small wave from across the room.

"Hi, Julia. You didn't tell me you worked as a personal assistant. You said you wanted to open a coffee shop."

"I do, but I have to work and save up to do that. Listen, if this is awkward for you, I can find another job. It's really not a big deal."

"No. It's not awkward. And I need someone now. Work is piling up."

"Okay. But just remember, it was only sex. No big deal," she said.

"I know that, and I'm not making a big deal about it. I'm just in shock that neither one of us knew it. Didn't Grayson tell you that you'd be working for me?"

"He told me I'd be working for Sam Kind, but you never told me your last name. And Sam is a very common name. I know five guys named Sam, and you're number six."

"I guess we didn't do much talking that night." I sighed.

"No. We didn't." The corners of her mouth curved upward.

"Follow me, and I'll show you around. By the way, what is your last name?"

"Benton."

"Welcome to Kind Design & Architecture, Miss Benton."

*Shit. Shit. Shit. My brothers were going to have a field day with this one.*

I led her to the space outside my office that consisted of a large L-shaped desk, file cabinets that lined the wall, an iMac computer, a phone, and a comfortable oversized leather office chair.

"This will be your workspace, and you'll need to be available at all times of the day and night. Just because normal work hours are eight to five everywhere else, it's not for me."

"That's fine. I'm used to it."

"Where did you work prior?"

"I was the personal assistant for Steven Hart over at Hart Industries."

"That's right. Grayson mentioned something about him highly recommending you. Wait a minute. Didn't he just shut down his business and pass away recently?"

"Yeah. He did."

"I'm sorry. How long did you work for him?"

"Three and a half years."

"And prior to that, you were a personal assistant to whom?" I cocked my head.

"I wasn't. I was the assistant manager at a coffee shop." She grinned.

I stared at her for a moment with narrowed eyes.

"Of course, you were. You have a weird relationship with coffee."

"You remembered. I'm impressed."

"How could I forget something like that when you went on a rant about me putting cream in my coffee." I gave her a smirk.

She let out a laugh.

"You don't have a secretary?" she asked.

"I share a secretary with my father. Her name is Joan, and she's amazing. Follow me, and I'll show our building division."

*I prayed Stefan wasn't in his office.*

"This is the building division that my brother, Stefan, runs. I design, and he manages the construction projects. Together, we oversee it all."

"What about your other two brothers? Do they work here as well?"

"No. Sebastian owns his own restaurant called *Four Kinds*, and Simon is a detective with the LAPD."

"Oh my God. I love that restaurant. The food is so good." She smiled. "Wow. That's your brother's place. Didn't he get the Michelin award or something?"

"Yes. He did."

"Hey, bro. Who's—Julia?" Stefan walked over.

"Hi, Stefan. It's good to see you again."

"You, too." His eye narrowed at me. "What's going on here?"

"Julia is the woman Grayson hired as my new personal assistant."

It took him a minute to process, and then he started laughing.

"I'm sorry. Wow, what a coincidence. Anyway, it's good to have you here, Julia. Keep this one in line." He patted my back.

"I'll do my best." The corners of her mouth curved upward.

"Follow me, and I'll take you to meet my father, the owner of the company."

When we reached his office, I lightly tapped on his door and opened it.

"Hey, son. Come in."

"Hey, Dad. I'd like you to meet Julia Benton, my new personal assistant. "Julia, this is my father, Henry Kind."

"Julia," he got up from his desk, "it's nice to meet you. Welcome to Kind Design & Architecture." He extended his hand to her.

"Thank you. It's nice to meet you, Mr. Kind."

"What happened to Kendra?" he asked.

"She got another job."

"Oh." His eyes narrowed at me because he knew I was lying. "I wasn't aware she'd given her notice."

I shifted my weight as my hands stayed tightly tucked in my pants pockets, and I pursed my lips. There was no doubt I was going to hear about this.

"We'll let you get back to work," I said.

"It was nice to meet you, Julia. Sam, I need to speak with you for a moment about that project you're working on."

*And here it came.*

"You can go back to my office. I'll be there in a few minutes." I turned and looked at Julia.

"Okay." She smiled. "It was nice to meet you, Mr. Kind."

As soon as Julia shut the door, my dad started in on me.

"You slept with Kendra, didn't you?"

"Dad, I—"

"I don't want to hear it, Sam." He put his hand up. "What have I told you time and time again about sleeping with the women at the office?"

"I know, but—"

"No buts!" His voice raised. "One of these days, we're going to get slapped with a sexual harassment suit because you can't keep your dick in your pants."

I wanted to tell him look who was talking, considering he'd cheated on all his ex-wives except my mother. But who the hell knew, he might have.

"I'm warning you. You are to stay away from Julia."

*Shit. If he only knew about Friday night.*

"That's going to be impossible since she's my personal assistant."

"Don't get smart with me, boy. You know exactly what I mean."

"Are we done here, Dad? I need to get back to work."

"Yes. We're done." He shook his head. "By the way, did you and your brothers go get your tuxedos yet for the wedding?"

"We're going tomorrow."

"Okay. I'll let Celeste know."

As soon as I left his office, I went to see Grayson. Stepping inside, I planted my hands firmly on his desk and stared at him while he finished his phone call.

"I have to call you back, Louise." He ended the call.

"How could you?" I spoke in a stern voice. "You blatantly lied to me!"

"She was the most qualified, Sam! Here, read the recommendation from Steven Hart." He handed me the letter.

Grabbing it from him, I stood there and read it.

"This is on you!" He pointed at me. "You need to learn to control your impulses around women!"

"Yeah. Well, it's too late!" I threw the letter on the desk.

"I kind of figured that by the look on both of your faces when you saw each other! If this is a problem, I'll move her somewhere else in the company. I just can't fire her because you slept with her."

"It won't be a problem, and it won't happen again. I can assure you of that. She's different."

"What do you mean by that?"

"The day after our night together, I told her it was only a one-time thing, and she agreed that it was for her as well."

"She could have a change of heart since she'll be working with you every day."

"Then I'll have to make sure she doesn't. Don't lie to me again!" I pointed at him as I walked out of his office.

# CHAPTER 9

*J*ulia

I sat at my desk and patiently waited for Sam to return. I should have put two and two together that night. His name and the house he lived in. It was different—a different design than all the other houses on the beach. I should have known he designed it himself. So much for my one-night stand and never seeing him again. Had I known, I would never have slept with him. I would admit that thoughts of him rumbled around in my head all weekend. The night we spent together was incredible, and I was just about over it until I saw him again.

"My office, now," he said.

Getting up from my desk, I followed him inside.

"Shut the door," he snapped.

"Is something wrong?" I asked.

He rubbed his forehead and let out a sigh.

"What happened between us the other night will never happen again. Do you understand me?"

I stood there in confusion because I had no idea where

this was coming from. I'd thought we already put that behind us.

"Yes. Of course, I understand. I don't plan on it ever happening again. I already told you that. You were a one-night stand, Sam. Nothing more."

He stood there and narrowed his eyes at me with his hands tucked in his pants pockets.

"Do you usually have a lot of one-night stands?" he asked.

"Well—I—I've had a few here and there. I'm human, and I have needs just like you."

"Fair enough, Julia. I apologize for my abruptness. I was just worried that—"

"That I would want more from you?"

"Well, yes."

"I don't understand that. Just because two people have casual sex, it doesn't mean anything. We had a good time for a few hours. That's all it was. So can we put it behind us and get to work?"

"Yes." The corners of his mouth curved upward. "Let's do that. Thank you, Julia."

"No need to thank me." I grinned. "I look forward to getting to know you better as a boss, and I will get you to stop putting that crap in your coffee." A smirk crossed my lips, and he chuckled.

"Never."

~

*I*t was an interesting first day of work. When I got home, I kicked off my heels, poured a glass of wine, and sat down on the couch to relax. Picking up my phone, I called my mom.

"Hello."

"Hi, Mom."

"Julia, sweetheart, how was your first day at your new job?"

"It was good and interesting."

"And your boss? What's he like?"

"He's nice. I think I'm going to like working for him."

"Good. I'm happy to hear that. Your father and I are going out to dinner tomorrow night, and we'd like you to join us."

"Sounds good. What time?"

"Seven o'clock?"

"Seven's good. Which restaurant are you going to?"

"We're not sure yet. I'll text you tomorrow when we decide on a place."

"Sounds good, Mom. I'll see you tomorrow night. Tell Dad I said hi."

"I will, Julia. Love you."

"Love you too."

Setting down my phone, I stood up and grabbed my wine glass. Walking over to the console table, I picked up the 5x7 frame and stared at it as tears filled my eyes. Suddenly, my phone rang and when I grabbed it, my sister, Jenni, was Face-timing me.

"Hey, you!" I smiled when I saw her face on the screen.

"Hi." She let out a long yawn.

"What time is it there? Like five a.m.?"

"Yep."

"Why are you up?"

"I have an early photoshoot." She climbed out of bed, went into the bathroom, and set her phone up against the back of the sink. "How was your first day at work?"

"It was good. There's something I have to tell you."

"Okay. Spill it." She put some toothpaste on her tooth-brush and began brushing her teeth.

"Remember the guy I told you about from Friday night?"

"Yeah. The hot one in the bar that lives in Venice on the beach?"

"Yep."

"Don't tell me he tracked you down and wants to go out."

"No. He didn't track me down. He's my new boss."

"What?! Hold on." She rinsed her toothbrush and mouth and placed her hands on the sink, so her face was mere inches from the phone. "You slept with your boss?"

"I didn't know he was my boss on Friday."

"Shit, Julia. That's fucked up."

"Yeah. I know." I bit my bottom lip.

"Did he freak out when he saw you?"

"Pretty much. But we talked about it, and things are cool now."

"From the way you described him, I have a feeling the two of you will be hitting the sheets again soon."

"Absolutely not. We already said it wouldn't happen again."

"If you say so. I have to go, or I'll be late. We'll talk later. I love you."

"I love you too. Have fun."

"Always do." She blew me a kiss.

# CHAPTER 10

*S*am

I was sitting out on my deck drinking a bottle of imported beer when Simon walked over.

"Hey, bro."

"Go grab a beer," I said.

He went inside, grabbed a beer, and took the seat next to me.

"So, I heard—"

"I don't want to talk about it," I spoke as I brought the bottle up to my lips.

He chuckled before taking a sip of his beer.

"Only you, Sam. Only you." He grinned as he shook his head.

"What are the odds? I mean, come on."

"Is she cool working for you?"

"Yeah. I guess. She told me that I was a one-night stand and nothing more. Can you believe that? No woman has ever said that to me."

"Maybe she was just saying that. You know how women are. Maybe she's putting on a front for your sake."

"I don't think so. I'm good at reading women, and she's different. She said it with such seriousness. There wasn't a hint of pretending going on with her."

"Okay. Then she's a rare one."

"I asked her if she usually has a lot of one-night stands."

"Wow. You asked her that? What did she say?"

"She said 'here and there' and then proceeded to tell me she was human and has needs."

"Hmm. Why is she single? I mean, look at her. She's a beautiful and sexy woman. Someone like her shouldn't be single. Unless she's crazy, and you just haven't seen it yet." He laughed.

"I have no clue. I didn't ask her. She's not crazy. In fact, she's overly nice. Like, sickening nice. Oh, and Dad laid into me about Kendra. He said we're going to end up getting slapped with a sexual harassment suit because I can't keep my dick in my pants."

"Damn. Like he's one to talk."

"Right? That's what I wanted to say to him. Then he warned me that I better stay away from Julia."

"Well, in all honesty, bro, you should. But I don't know how you're going to. She's hot, she's overly nice, and she's your personal assistant. Good luck with that." He held his bottle up to me.

"I can do it. I already know what she has under those sexy clothes she wears. I'm good." I tapped my bottle against his.

"Hey, what's going on over here?" Stefan asked as he walked up.

"Just some brotherly talk," Simon spoke. "Go grab a beer and join us."

"Is Sebastian at the restaurant?" I asked.

"Yeah. He wants us to come by tomorrow night for dinner. He's testing out a new dish."

"Why are we always the guinea pigs?" Simon smirked.

"So, how was your day with Julia?" Stefan grinned as he sat down on the other side of me.

"It was fine."

"Why is she single?" he asked.

"I asked the same damn thing," Simon spoke.

"Why the hell are we all single?" I asked as I looked at them.

"You know why," Stefan said. "Mom and Dad fucked us up with all of their relationship woes. Who the hell needs that shit in their life?"

"True, brother. So true," Simon said as he finished his beer. "I have to go. There's a new case I'm working on, and I want to follow up on a lead. Don't forget about tomorrow. Twelve o'clock at the tuxedo place."

"We'll be there," Stefan said. "You know, we should just buy the damn tuxedos. We've stood up in every one of Dad's weddings. I'm pretty sure this won't be the last one."

"I don't know. He really seems to love Celeste." I glanced over at him.

"He really loved Mom, Delaney, Madeline, and Anna too. I have to go too, bro. Nanny Kate is off-duty soon." He held his fist out.

"I'll talk to you later." I fist-bumped him.

Taking the last sip of my beer, I went inside and got another one. I couldn't stop thinking about Julia no matter how hard I tried, and I wondered what she was doing. Was she out? Perhaps scoping out her next one-night stand? Was she at home alone? Was she with a friend? Shit. I needed to find an excuse to talk to her. Pulling my phone from my pocket, I dialed her number.

"Hello."

"Julia, It's Sam."

"Hey, Sam. How are you?"

"I'm good. I need you in the office tomorrow morning at

seven. I want to go over some things I need you to do regarding the project I'm working on."

"Okay. I'll be there."

"Great. Um. Have you had dinner yet?"

"I just took out a chicken dish I made from the oven. Why?"

"Nothing. I was just going to grab a burger, and since we were talking, I thought if you hadn't eaten yet, you could join me."

"Oh. You're more than welcome to come over and try my chicken dish, if you want. I have plenty."

"No. That's okay. Thanks. I'll see you tomorrow morning."

"Okay. See you in the morning."

"Enjoy the rest of your evening."

"You too, Sam."

As tempting as it was to go over there, I shouldn't be doing shit like that. A restaurant was different. We would be surrounded by people and not confined alone in her apartment.

"Good morning." Julia beamed as she walked into my office with a container in one hand and a cup holder with two cups of coffee in the other.

"Good morning." The corners of my mouth curved upward.

"I brought you a coffee and something else." She grinned as she handed me the plastic container.

"What is this?"

"Open it and find out." The smile never left her face.

I removed the lid from the container, and inside were three apple turnovers.

"Wow. Thank you. Where did you get them from?"

"I made them."

"You made these?" My brow arched as I pointed to the turnovers.

"Yeah. I made them last night after dinner."

"From scratch?"

"Yes. From scratch." She let out a laugh. "I brought one for your dad and Stefan."

"Thank you. That was nice of you. Did you by any chance get some cream for the coffee?"

"No. I did not." Her eye narrowed.

"That's okay. There's some in the refrigerator in the break room."

"Note to self: throw out the creamer."

"Don't you dare." I pointed at her as the corners of my mouth curved upward.

"So, why did you bring me in so early?"

I picked up a brown folder from my desk and handed it to her.

"Inside, you'll find the documentation for all the permits we'll need for the new project I'm working on. I need you to type it all up, and when you're done, I'll look it over, and then I'll have you take it to the city building for submission. Every day you'll learn a new task that you'll have to do every time I take on a new design project. It'll become automatic for you."

"Okay. I'll go get started." She smiled.

"I need you to do something for me first."

"Okay."

"Go to the breakroom, grab the creamer from the fridge, and bring it to me."

I watched as she inhaled a deep breath.

"Got it. I'll be right back."

While she was getting my creamer, I picked up a turnover and bit into it. Holy shit.

"Here's your creamer," she said as she walked back into my office.

"Julia, this—this is the best damn turnover I've ever had."

"Thank you. I'm happy you like it." A wide grin crossed her lips.

"No. I don't like it. I love it. How long have you been making these?"

"This was my first time. I've never made them before. I looked up some recipes, tweaked some of the ingredients, and added a couple of my own."

"Well, these are way better than the ones from the café across the street."

"Thanks, Sam."

I pulled the lid from my coffee cup and picked up the carton of creamer.

"If you'll excuse me, I'm going to get to work on those permits. I can't bear to see you do that." She put her hand up and walked out.

I couldn't help but chuckle.

"Hey, Sam. I have the — are those apple turnovers?" Stefan walked into my office.

"Yes. Take one. Julia made them last night. One for me, you, and Dad."

"She bakes?"

"I guess."

He took one from the container and bit into it. He had the same look on his face as I did.

"Holy shit. These are delicious. Julia," he shouted, "these turnovers are amazing. Thank you."

"You're welcome, Stefan."

"Where did that woman come from? She's gorgeous, overly nice, and she bakes. I bet she's amazing in bed. Tell me, is she?"

"You get that fucking thought out of your head right now." I pointed at him.

"Fine. Thought gone. Anyway, we need to go inspect the Shores building now that it's finally completed. We can go after our fittings for our tuxes."

"Okay. Sounds good."

We both looked at the last turnover.

"Want to split this?" I asked him.

"Isn't that one for Dad?"

"Does he really need it? He is getting married soon, and he's been watching what he's eating."

"True. And he has been working out every day," Stefan said. "Yeah. He doesn't need it."

I picked up the turnover, broke it in half, and gave Stefan his piece.

"Man, do you think she has anymore?" he asked.

"I don't know. Ask her when you leave. Do me a favor and put this creamer back in the refrigerator."

"Sure thing. I know it's been killing you sitting on your desk." He smirked.

# CHAPTER 11

*J*ulia

"Shit!" I heard Sam yell from his office. "Julia!"

Getting up from my seat, I went to see what he wanted.

"What's wrong?"

"I don't have my wallet. I need you to drive to my house, get it, and bring it to me at the place where my brothers and I are getting fitted for our tuxedos for my father's wedding. I don't have time to go get it myself."

"Sure. Okay. How do I get in?"

He reached into his pants pocket and pulled out his keys.

"Take my keys. I'll have one made for you because I'll be sending you over there for different things occasionally."

"You don't need your car key to go to the tuxedo place?"

"No. I'll have Stefan drive. We have to do a final inspection on a building after anyway."

"Okay."

"You better go now." He looked at his watch. "I'll text you the address of the shop we'll be at."

I grabbed my purse and headed to my car. When I arrived

at Sam's house, I went up to his bedroom and grabbed his wallet from the dresser. Looking around his room, it was as clean as a whistle. Too clean for a bachelor. I was curious because the night I was here, I noticed it was overly clean and organized. Opening the door to his walk-in closet, it was bigger than my bedroom, with custom-built racks, drawers, and slide outs. In the middle sat a custom-made piece with large slide-out drawers and covered with an Italian marble top. His suits hung perfectly and were divided by designer and color on the top rack, with his dress shirts which were also arranged by color on the rack below. In the center, there was a brass handle attached to what appeared to be a pull-out drawer of some kind. Walking over to it, I grabbed hold of the handle, and when I pulled it, the inside was filled with different ties, all hung perfectly by color. On the wall across from his suits, his dress shoes were showcased as if they were on display at a store. Damn. And I thought I had a lot of shoes. I left that closet and walked over to the other set of doors next to it. It was the exact same layout, but instead of suits, all his causal clothes were perfectly hung, ranging from casual shirts and pants to sportswear with the opposite wall showcasing his casual shoes and sneakers.

Looking at my watch, I needed to go. As I was locking the door, I heard a voice behind me.

"Who are you?"

Turning around, I saw an adorable little girl standing there with curly blonde hair.

"I'm Julia." I smiled at her. "Who are you?"

"Lily. Why are you at my Uncle Sam's house when he's not home?"

"I'm your uncle's personal assistant, and I came to get his wallet for him. How old are you, Lily?"

"Eight."

"May I ask who your dad is?"

"His name is Stefan. You probably know him since he works with my uncle."

"I do know your dad. He's a very nice man. Shouldn't you be in school?"

"There is no school today."

"Oh. I see. Well, it was nice to meet you. You're not home alone, are you?" I furrowed my brows.

"No. Nanny Kate is there. She's making my lunch."

"Lily? Who are you talking to?" An older woman walked over.

"Nanny Kate, this is Julia, Uncle Sam's personal assistant. Julia, this is Nanny Kate."

"It's nice to meet you, Julia." She smiled.

"And you as well, Nanny Kate. I wish I could stay and chat, but Sam is waiting for his wallet." I held it up.

"Well, we won't keep you. Come on, Lily. Let's go have lunch."

"Bye, Julia." Lily smiled and waved goodbye.

"Bye, Lily." I waved.

I was on my way to the tuxedo shop when my phone dinged with a text message from Sam.

*"Where are you?"*

*"I'm almost there."*

After finding a place to park, I ran into the shop with Sam's wallet in my hand.

"Here." I handed it to him as he was getting measured.

"What the hell took you so long?"

"As I was leaving, I got stopped by your niece."

"Ah, you met Lily?" Stefan smiled as he walked over.

"I did. She's adorable. I didn't know you had a daughter."

"Yeah. That kid is the love of my life."

"Hi there, I'm Sebastian, Sam's other brother."

"And I'm Simon."

"It's nice to meet both of you." I grinned.

I gulped as I stood there and stared at the four of them together. It was a total ovary explosion moment, for they were all so incredibly sexy.

"Is there anywhere else you need me to run before I head back to the office?" I asked Sam.

"No. I just need you to get back and finish that paperwork for the permits and building contracts."

"I already finished them." I pulled the file from my oversized purse. "If you want to look them over now, I can run to the city building on my way back to the office."

"Okay, then." His lips gave way to a smile as he took the folder from me.

While his brothers were getting measured, Sam sat down on the leather couch inside the shop and looked them over.

"Everything looks great." He closed the folder and handed it back to me.

"Then I'm off. I'll see you when I get back to the office. It was nice to meet you, Sebastian and Simon." I smiled.

"Good to meet you too, Julia. See you around."

# CHAPTER 12

*S*am

"Damn," Sebastian said as he watched Julia walk out of the shop.

"Keep your eyes to yourself and off my personal assistant. The only one who's allowed to stare at her is me."

"You're lucky, bro," Simon spoke as he patted my shoulder. "She takes a personal assistant to a whole new level."

"Okay. Enough about Julia. If we're done here, Stefan and I need to go inspect a building."

"Don't forget you're coming to dinner at the restaurant. Seven o'clock, sharp."

"We'll be there," I said.

After our inspection, Stefan and I headed back to the office.

"Any messages?" I asked Julia as I stopped at her desk.

"Mr. Kramer called and said to call him ASAP. He said he tried your cell, but you didn't answer."

"Yeah. I got his voice message. I'll call him right now. How did it go at the city building?"

"It went great. Grace told me to tell you that you never

responded to the text messages she sent a week ago, and she doesn't appreciate being ignored." She folded her hands on her desk while a smirk crossed her beautiful lips.

I let out a sigh and went into my office. Pulling my phone from my pocket, I called Ken Kramer.

"It's about time, Sam."

"Sorry, Ken. I was at an inspection. What's up?"

"I need you to meet me at 311 Sunset Blvd in Venice. There's something I want to talk to you about."

"Okay. I'm on my way."

"Good. See you soon."

"Julia, I have to run out and meet a client, and then I'm going to work from home. When you're finished with your work, you can go home for the day."

"Did you make nice with Grace?"

I stopped dead in my tracks, turned around, and looked at her.

"Why are you asking me that?"

"Why are you answering a question with a question? If you have no intention of seeing her again, just tell her."

"I—" I inhaled a sharp breath. "Don't you worry about Grace," I said.

As I turned and headed towards the elevator, I heard her laugh.

Driving down Sunset Blvd, I saw Ken standing on the corner in front of a building. After finding a place to park, I climbed out of the car and headed down the street to meet him.

"Why are we here?" I shook his hand.

"See this building? It's been vacant for over a year."

"Yeah. I know. It's odd the owner never put anything in," I spoke.

"He recently passed away, and I want this building. I've wanted it for a long time."

"Who owns it?"

"His name was Steven Hart. When I saw that the antique shop was closing over a year ago, I got in touch with Steven and asked him if he was interested in selling me the building. I made him a very generous offer, and he said no. He told me he had other plans for it. Then, when I found out he was ill and he was terminal, I approached him again. He told me the same thing, and he refused to sell. I don't know why. Especially since the man was dying. You'd think he'd want the money for his wife. Little by little, he started selling off pieces of his company. So, I paid him another visit about the building, and he still told me no."

"That's strange." I furrowed my brows. "Who owns the building now that he's deceased?"

"I don't know. I'm sure he left everything to his wife. They never had any children."

"So, go to his wife and make her an offer she can't refuse."

"I already tried. She told me she knows nothing about the building and to speak with Steven's attorney."

"Did you?"

"I did. He said the building is in Steven's trust, and the will is being sent to probate and will be ready in a couple of months. So, in the meantime, I want to get designs ready for when I buy it. I know he left it to his wife, and they're just not saying. What the hell is she going to do with an empty building? I'll swoop in, make her an offer she can't refuse, and take it off her hands. I'm going to get the blueprints from the city. While I'm doing that, I want you to get to work on redesigning the outside. Once I get my hands on the blueprints, I'll bring them to you, and we'll look them over and start making a plan."

"What are you putting in here?"

"My wife wants to relocate her shop, and she wants this building."

"Happy wife, happy life." I smiled.

"No shit." He shook his head. "I've done the research and had my guys put some numbers together. Between the location, tourists, and foot traffic, this place will be a gold mine for us."

"Okay," I said as I pulled my phone from my pocket and snapped some pictures.

"I want designs in place so we can start right away when I get the building."

"I'll get to work on it, Ken." I extended my hand.

"Thanks, Sam." He reached out and shook my hand. "I'll be in touch."

Climbing into my car, I sat there for a moment and thought about what Julia had said about Grace, so I decided to call her and give her another assignment before the day was over.

"Hello."

"Are you on your way home yet?"

"I'm just leaving the building."

"Good. I want you to stop by the city building on your way home and give Grace a message from me."

There was silence on the other end.

"I'm listening," she spoke.

"Tell her I'm very busy, and I won't be calling her again."

"You can't be serious."

"I am. You're my personal assistant, and this is what I need you to assist me with."

"Fine. I'll see you tomorrow."

"Enjoy your evening, Miss Benton."

All I heard was a click.

# CHAPTER 13

*J*ulia

I couldn't believe that man was having me do his dirty work. After finding a parking spot in the parking garage, I entered the city building and took the elevator up to the third floor.

"Julia, you're back." Grace smiled.

*Damn him.*

"Hi, Grace. I gave Sam your message."

"And?"

"I think it's best that you don't expect him to call. He's very busy."

"He sure as hell wasn't busy the night he fucked me." She cocked her head, and I swallowed hard. "He sent you here, didn't he?"

"Yes, and I'm so sorry. You seem like a nice woman, and you don't need someone like Sam Kind and all the drama he brings. I'd take this as a win if I were you."

"What do you mean a 'win?'"

"He's rich, sexy, and you snagged him for one night. That's all you needed from him, and it's time to move on and find someone who isn't such a jerk. Come on, Grace, deep down you knew he wouldn't call you."

"I suppose I did." She looked down. "It is a win, isn't it?"

"Definitely." I smiled at her.

"Thanks, Julia."

"You're welcome. He's not worthy of you."

I walked out of the building and let out a deep breath. That would be the one and only time I'd do that for him. As I was driving home, a call came through from my mom.

"Hey, Mom."

"Hi, Julia. There's been a change in the restaurant tonight. Your father doesn't feel like Mexican."

"Oh. Okay. Where are we meeting?"

"Four Kinds in Venice. Your father called and made reservations for an outside table."

"Great. I'll see you there."

~

*J* was ten minutes late due to traffic and the fact that trying to find a parking spot wasn't easy. As the hostess led me through the restaurant, I heard someone call my name.

"Julia?"

Turning around, I saw Sebastian.

"Hi." I gave him a smile.

"Hi. You're dining here tonight?"

"Yeah. I'm meeting my parents."

"That's great. Which table?" he asked the hostess.

"Outside, table 7," she replied.

"I'll take her. Follow me." He smiled.

As we approached the table my parents were sitting at, my father stood up and kissed my cheek.

"Hello, sweetheart."

"Hi, Dad. Mom. I'd like you to meet Sebastian Kind. He owns the restaurant. Sebastian, these are my parents, Jerry and Diane Benton."

"It's nice to meet you." He extended his hand to my father and then to my mother.

"This is a wonderful restaurant," my father spoke. "Excellent food."

"Thank you. Your dinner is on me tonight."

"That's nice of you, but I couldn't." My father raised his hand.

"I insist. I'll have your waitress bring over a bottle of our finest wine. It was nice to meet you both."

"Thank you, Sebastian." I smiled.

"You're welcome. Enjoy."

I took my seat and placed my napkin on my lap.

My mother's lips gave way to a smirk. "Have you been holding out on us, Julia? How do you know that handsome man?"

"No, Mom. I haven't been holding out on you. He's my boss's brother. In fact, he has two other brothers as well. They're quadruplets."

"No shit," my father spoke.

"We had our hands full with you and your sister. I couldn't imagine juggling four children at once."

I reached in the basket and pulled out a piece of bread. As I looked up, I saw Sam walking towards our table with a smile on his face.

"Hello there. My brother told me you were here. I'm Sam Kind, Julia's boss." He extended his hand to my father.

"It's nice to meet you, Sam. I'm Jerry, and this is my wife, Diane."

"I can see where Julia gets her looks from." The corners of his mouth curved upward as he shook my mother's hand.

I couldn't help but roll my eyes.

"We'd love for you to join us," my father told him.

"As much as I'd love to, I'm here with my other brothers. Sebastian is testing out a new dish, and we're his Guinea pigs." A smirk crossed his face. "I just wanted to come over and say hi. Enjoy your dinner."

"Thanks, Sam." I smiled.

The moment he walked away, my mother placed her hand on mine and gave it a squeeze.

"That man is gorgeous. You didn't mention that when I asked you about him. Is he single?"

"Mom. Don't."

"Diane, leave it alone."

"Is it so wrong that I want my daughter to be happy?"

"I am happy, Mom."

"I know it's coming up, and I hate that your sister is in Europe. Why don't you take the day off work? We can shop all day, and you can spend the night."

"I can't take the day off. I'll be fine."

"It's been four years, Julia, and you haven't even so much as mentioned a man to us."

"Diane, please," my dad said. "Leave our daughter alone. When she's ready, she'll let us know. Isn't that right, sweetheart?"

"Yeah, Dad. I will. If you'll excuse me for a moment, I need to use the restroom."

After I washed my hands, I opened the door and saw Sam leaning up against the wall across from the bathroom with one hand tucked into his pants pockets.

"Oh, hey," I said.

"Did you take care of that errand earlier?"

"I did."

"And?"

"And what?"

"What did she say?"

"Not much. She's good."

"Really? She didn't give you any trouble?"

"No." I laughed. "Why would she?"

"I don't know." He shrugged.

"She's good, Sam." I patted his chest. "I'll see you tomor-row." I walked away.

"Wait, Julia."

"Yes?" I turned around.

"Do you know anything about a building that Steven owned on Sunset Blvd in Venice?"

"No. I can't say that I do. Why?"

"A client of mine wants the building. He wanted to buy it from Steven when he was alive, and he wouldn't sell. So now he's just waiting on Steven's trust to come out of probate. He's positive he left the building to his wife."

"I'm not sure why he'd do that."

"What do you mean?"

"What would she want with one of his buildings? She never got involved in any of his business matters. But who knows, maybe he did, and he had his reasons."

"If he did leave it to her, do you think she'd sell?"

"Definitely. I'm sure your client will be able to offer her a price, and she'll accept."

"We're hoping. Go enjoy the rest of your dinner with your parents. I'll see you in the morning." The corners of his mouth curved upward.

"Have a good night, Sam."

# CHAPTER 14

S am

"Having a little rendezvous with Julia in the bathroom?" Stefan smirked.

"I'm telling Sebastian you're fucking in his bathroom." Simon punched me in the arm.

"Shut the hell up. There was no rendezvous. I was just asking her about a building her former employer owned that one of our clients wants."

"The building Ken wants?" Stefan asked.

"Yeah. She knows nothing about it."

"That's strange." Stefan furrowed his brows. "She was his personal assistant. She should know something."

"Not if he kept it out of the office and from her," I said.

"Well, what say you, brothers?" Sebastian smiled as he walked over to our table.

"Honestly, this is one of the best dishes I've ever had."

"Yeah. Great job, bro," Stefan said.

"Absolutely. Now I feel like I can bring a girl here on a date." Simon smirked.

Sebastian picked up a piece of bread from the basket and threw it at him.

"I'm going to head home. I want to get started on Ken's project without any distractions," I said as I stood up from my chair.

"You mean without Julia around to distract you." A smirk crossed Stefan's lips.

"Don't you have to get home to Nanny Kate and Lily?"

"Yeah. I better. I promised Lily we'd build a fort in the living room tonight."

"You're the best daddy ever!" Simon exclaimed.

"Damn right I am." Stefan pointed at him.

~

*W*hen I arrived home, I poured a drink and took it over to my drafting table in my office. Pulling out my phone, I saw I had a text message from Grace. Sighing, I took a seat behind my desk and opened it.

*"I just wanted you to know that you're a dick, and I'm an amazing woman who deserves better. You may think you're cool getting me into bed and then ghosting me, but the reality is, Sam, I'm the winner here because I realized that you're an egotistical man-whore who doesn't respect women. Enjoy your miserable life, douchebag."*

Rolling my eyes, I took a screenshot of her text message and then blocked her. What the hell did Julia say to her? This warranted a phone call.

"Hello."

"Julia, it's Sam."

"Yes. I know. Your name appeared on my phone."

"What did you say to Grace today?"

"I told her you were very busy and wouldn't be calling her. Why?"

I cleared my throat and began to read the text message she'd sent. Julia couldn't contain her laughter, and it was pissing me off.

"Damn. I didn't know little Grace had it in her." She continued to laugh.

"So again, what did you say to her? Did you tell her she deserved better?"

"Yes. Because she does. I'm sorry, Sam, but this is your fault. You didn't have the balls to tell her yourself, and you sent me to do your dirty work. I didn't want to hurt her feelings and make her feel used and worthless. Because that's exactly how you made her feel. So, I'm not sorry for the things I said to her."

"Have you forgotten to whom you're speaking to?"

"No." She laughed. "I'm sorry. I still can't get over what Grace said to you."

"Goodnight, Julia."

"Goodnight, Sam."

I ended the call, got up from my chair, and went to my drafting table. I always liked to draw my designs by hand first, then do it on my computer. As I was looking over the photos I took and trying to come up with an idea for the front, my phone rang, and it was my friend, Casey Connors.

"Hey, Case. What's up, my friend?"

"Hey, Sam. Sorry to call so late. The day got away from me. I just bought the land next door to the house in Montauk, and we want to expand."

"Let me guess. You need an architect?"

"You got it. And I want only the best. What do you say? Interested?"

"Definitely. When do you want me to come out?"

"This weekend if possible."

"I can fly out on Friday afternoon."

"Sounds good. Our flight from Hawaii gets in Friday

around three p.m. So, we'll be home around five-thirty or six, depending on traffic. No need to get a room somewhere. You'll stay in our guesthouse. It's been a while, my friend, and we have some serious catching up to do."

"We sure do. Thanks, Casey."

"Don't mention it. I'll give John, our property manager, a call and have him stock the fridge and leave a key for you in case you get there before we do."

~

"Morning, Julia. Can you come into my office?" I spoke as I walked past her desk.

"Good morning."

"I need you to book two first-class tickets to New York City for Friday. And then I need you to book a rental car at the airport. I want an SUV. Mercedes, Land Rover, Cadillac. Something nice and comfortable."

"Okay. For you and which brother? Stefan?"

"You and me." My lips gave way to a smirk.

"Excuse me?"

"You're coming with me. My friend, Casey, just bought some land next to his house in Montauk, and he wants to expand. He asked me if I could come out and draw up some plans."

"And you need me to go? Why?" She cocked her head.

"Because you're my personal assistant, and I'm going to need assisting. I would take Stefan, but this is Nanny Kate's weekend off, and my mother is going away for the weekend with her husband, and my father is too busy with the wedding. Casey told me to stay in the guesthouse. But don't worry, there are two bedrooms."

"I'm not worried at all," she spoke in a serious tone. "Which airport?"

"LaGuardia is fine. Then we'll drive the three hours to Montauk. Make sure to pack some warmer clothes. It's quite chilly there this time of year."

"And when are we coming back?"

"Book the return flight for Sunday. We'll head back to the city on Saturday. There's a new building going up by a friend of mine I want to see, and then we'll grab some dinner. In fact, book a suite at the Mandarin Oriental for each of us for one night. Or you could book one suite with two bedrooms. It's up to you."

"Okay. I'll get working on it now." She turned and headed towards the door.

"Julia?"

She turned and looked at me.

"It'll be fun." The corners of my mouth curved upward.

Her lips gave way to a small smile before walking out of my office.

I had my reasons for bringing her with me, one of them being that I wanted to get to know her better. And the best way to do that was to be alone with her without any distractions or disruptions by members of my family or work. I knew what I was doing. Maybe it wasn't the smartest decision on my part, but I didn't care. Julia Benton had my attention since the moment I saw her in the café that morning, and I wanted to know more about her.

"Hey." Stefan blew into my office. "Can you watch Lily on Saturday? I have a date with Melinda."

"Who?" My brows furrowed.

"Just some girl I met the other night when I was out with Grayson. She was with her friends, so I got her number and told her we'd go out this weekend."

"As nice as that sounds, I can't. I'm going out of town."

"Where the hell are you going, and why didn't you mention it to any of us?"

"Casey just called me last night. He bought the property next to his house in Montauk. He's expanding and wants me to design it. I told him I could fly out Friday."

"Shit. Do you think Mom will watch her?"

"Mom and Curtis are going to Vegas for the weekend, remember?"

"That's right." He sighed. "I'll ask Sebastian or Simon. It's Nanny Kate's weekend off, and she's done a lot for me this week already, so I don't want to ask her. Are you going alone?" His eye narrowed at me.

"No. I'm taking Julia."

"I knew it!" His finger pointed at me. "You promised Dad and Grayson you'd stay away from her. But I knew you wouldn't. If she quits, Sam—"

"She's not going to quit. I already told you she's different."

"Yeah, yeah. I'm heading out for a couple of hours. I'll talk to you later."

# CHAPTER 15

*J*ulia

Of all the weekends for him to plan a trip and make me go with him, this wasn't the one. After making the reservations, I got up from my seat and walked into his office.

"All reservations are made. They only had one suite available at the Mandarin."

"A two-bedroom?" he asked.

"Yes. And I booked a car rental and the last two first-class seats."

"Excellent. It'll be a good trip." The corners of his mouth curved upward.

I knew what he was thinking or hoping for, and I would sleep with him again without a doubt. Once you've had what Sam had to offer, it was hard not to want more. But this wasn't the weekend for that. I needed to keep myself in check and remember this was a business trip and not let my emotions get the best of me.

After work, I climbed in my car and headed to my mom and dad's house because I wanted to tell them I was leaving on Friday. When I stepped inside, I saw my father sitting in his favorite chair in the living room.

"Hi, Daddy." I smiled as I walked over and kissed his cheek.

"Hi, sweetheart. What a pleasant surprise. I didn't know you were stopping by."

"Who are you—Julia, honey. I didn't know you were stopping by," my mom said as she hugged me.

"I really can't stay. I have to get home and do laundry because I'm leaving for a business trip with Sam on Friday."

"Where are you going?" my mom asked.

"New York City."

"Can't you tell him—"

"No, Mom. I can't. He's my boss, and if he says he needs me to go to New York with him, I have to go. It's probably for the best anyway. It'll keep me distracted."

"Well, I think it's a good idea," my dad spoke. "It'll do you good to get out of Los Angeles for the weekend."

~

*A*s we walked through the airport, I couldn't help but notice how the women looked at Sam. Horny women who wanted to devour him and the daggers in their eyes when they looked at me. I simply smiled because I'd had him, and I wanted to tell them he was everything they were fantasizing about.

"You're not a nervous flier, are you?" Sam glanced at me.

"No. Are you?"

"Not at all." A smirk crossed his lips.

As we were on our way to our gate, my eyes locked on a familiar face as he walked by.

"Girl…" He grinned.

71

"Oh my God, Jasper!" I let go of my carry-on and threw my arms around his neck.

"I can't believe this. I was going to call you." He hugged me tight.

"What are you doing in L.A.?" I asked.

"I'm moving back. I gave Atlanta and Garrison a year, and things didn't work out."

"Oh no. I'm sorry. Why didn't you tell me you were moving back?"

"I wanted to surprise you. Where are you flying off to?"

"New York. Jasper, this is my boss, Sam Kind. Sam, this is Jasper Huntley, a friend of mine."

"It's nice to meet you, Sam." He extended his hand.

"Nice to meet you too, Jasper."

"You're not working for Steven anymore?"

"He passed away a few weeks ago."

"I'm sorry, Jules." He pulled me into him. "We have a lot of catching up to do. When you get back from New York, call me, and we'll hit the town together."

"I definitely will. Where are you living?"

"I'm crashing with Blake until I find my own place."

"Awesome. You're just around the block from Jenni and me."

"How is that sister of yours?"

"She's good. She's in Europe right now doing a fashion shoot."

"Lucky girl. I need to get my luggage. We'll chat soon." He hugged me one last time. "Have fun in New York."

"Thanks, Jasper."

He headed toward baggage claim, and we continued to our gate.

"How do you know him?" Sam asked.

"We worked together at the coffee shop and have been friends ever since."

As soon as we took our seats in first class, a woman wearing tight leggings and a sports bra boarded the plane and proceeded to put her carry-on up in the overhead compartment.

"Here, let me help you with that," Sam said as he stood up.

"Thank you. You're very sweet." Her lips gave way to a flirtatious smile.

I swear I could feel the vomit rise in my throat. After helping her, he sat back in his seat and noticed me staring at him.

"What?"

"Did you help her because you're a nice guy or because her ass was practically planted in your face?"

"Are you jealous?" A smirk crossed his lips.

"Absolutely not."

"If I recall, I also helped you with your bag."

Before I could make a remark, my phone rang. Pulling it from my purse, I saw Jenni was Facetiming me.

"Hi." I smiled when I answered her call.

"Hey, you! I was hoping I'd catch you before you took off. I meant to call you earlier, but I couldn't get to my phone. How are you?"

"I'm good. Jenni, this is my boss, Sam. Sam, my sister Jenni." I held my phone out.

"Hi, Jenni. Nice to meet you."

"Nice to meet you too, Sam." She grinned. "Listen, I have to run. Have a safe flight."

"Thanks, sis. I'll talk to you later."

The second I ended the call, a text message from her came through.

*"He's sexy as hell, Julia. I didn't want to say anything over Facetime, but are you okay?"*

*"I'm fine, Jenni."*

*"I wish I was there with you. I talked to Mom last night, and she's concerned."*

*"When isn't she? Everyone needs to stop worrying about me and bringing it up. I'm fine."*

*"I know you are, sis. Have a safe flight. I love you."*

*"I love you too."*

I let out a sigh as I set my phone on airplane mode.

"Everything okay?" Sam asked.

"Yeah. Of course." I gave him a small smile.

"May I get you something to drink?" the flight attendant asked me.

"I'll have a glass of white wine."

"And for you, sir?"

"Single malt scotch, please. If you have it."

"We do." She smiled.

The next thing I knew, the woman across from Sam placed her hand on his arm.

"Thank you again for your assistance with my bag. I'm Lyndsey."

"I'm Sam, and you're welcome." He grinned.

"Your wife is very pretty."

"Oh. She's not my wife. She's my personal assistant."

"I take it you're going on a business trip?"

"Yes. We are."

"How about you?" he asked her.

"I'm flying home. I was in L.A. visiting a friend. Which hotel are you staying at? Maybe I can meet you at the bar, and we can have a drink together. Hey, sweetie. Would you mind switching seats with me?" she asked.

"Not at all." I smiled because I couldn't take it anymore.

As I went to get up, Sam firmly grabbed my arm.

"Sit down. I'm sorry, but she's staying where she is," he said to Lyndsey. "Now, if you'll excuse me, I need to have a conversation with my assistant."

She gave him a look of disapproval and turned her head.

"What the hell do you think you were doing?" he asked quietly.

"I didn't mind switching seats with her."

"Well, I do."

As soon as we were in the air, Sam pulled out his laptop and did some design work while I pulled out my kindle from my purse and began reading. I found it difficult to concentrate because thoughts of tomorrow popped into my head. As hard as I tried not to think about it, I couldn't help it. Tears began to form in my eyes, and I took in a deep breath and discreetly wiped them.

"Are you crying?" Sam asked.

I couldn't lie to him because clearly, he could see I was.

"A little bit. This part in the book I'm reading is sad."

"Oh. Okay." He turned back to his laptop.

When the plane landed, we both stood up, and Sam was nice enough to let Lyndsey out first.

"After you." He gestured.

"Thank you. And by the way, I rescind my offer for that drink."

I couldn't help but snicker.

"That's okay. I wasn't going to take you up on it anyway. If I'm going to have a drink with a beautiful woman, it will be with my assistant."

"Typical asshole," she said as she exited the plane.

"That wasn't very nice," I said to Sam.

"Too bad. She's a bitch and needed to be knocked down a few notches. Besides, you should be flattered."

"I am, oh godly one." I placed my hand over my heart.

"Very funny." He shook his head.

As we walked to the car rental area, I looked out the windows and noticed it had started to rain.

"I didn't know it was raining here?"

"I guess they're calling for some bad storm today. Hopefully, we can stay ahead of it to Montauk."

A knot formed in the pit of my stomach, and I started to break out in a sweat.

"Maybe we should grab something to eat before we head out," I said.

"Why? We can eat much better food outside of the airport."

"But we can grab something quick here. Please, Sam."

# CHAPTER 16

*S* am

Between the pleading in her voice and the pleading in her eyes, I couldn't say no. But I couldn't understand why she'd want to eat at the airport.

"Fine. We can grab something here." My lips formed a small smile.

"There's a Shake Shack right over here. We can grab a couple of burgers," she said.

"Okay. Shake Shack it is."

I stood in line and ordered our food while Julia went and grabbed us a table. Setting the tray down, I took the seat across from her.

"Your burger, fries, and coke, Miss Benton."

"Thank you, Mr. Kind."

"I don't want to rush you, but I really want to get on the road and get to Montauk."

"If a storm is on its way, maybe we should just stay at a hotel for the night and head there tomorrow."

"We'll be fine. Besides, Casey is expecting us tonight. Are you afraid of the rain or something?" I furrowed my brows.

"No." She frowned as she picked up her coke and took a sip. "But storms can be bad, and people shouldn't be driving in them."

"I'm a good driver, and we'll be fine."

My phone rang, and when I pulled it from my pocket, I saw Casey was calling."

"Hey, Case."

"Hey, Sam. Listen, our flight is delayed a couple of hours because of some storms out on the east coast. Are you already in New York?"

"Yeah. We just landed not too long ago."

"Just go to the house and make yourselves comfortable. I'll let you know when we board. I'm sorry, man."

"Don't worry about it. I'll take a look around and see what I can come up with, and we'll go over it when you arrive."

"Thanks, Sam. I'll be in touch."

"What's wrong?" Julia asked.

"Casey's flight is delayed a couple of hours because of the storms. If you're finished, we should get going."

"Yeah. I'm done."

We threw our trash away and headed to the car rental counter.

"You're all set, Mr. Kind. Your car is waiting for you with the keys inside in spot 310."

"Thank you."

When we approached spot 310, sitting there was a black Land Rover Discovery.

"This will do," I said as I opened the trunk and put our bags inside.

Once I started the vehicle, I punched in Casey's address on the GPS.

"According to the GPS, it's about a two hour and twenty-minute drive if we don't hit any major traffic."

"Ha. This is New York. The traffic is way worse here than L.A."

"Yeah, you're probably right." I sighed.

"You must be excited for your dad's wedding," Julia said.

"Umm. No, I'm not. None of us are."

"Why? Don't you like his fiancée?"

"Celeste is nice. We're just tired of standing up for him."

"What do you mean?"

"This is his fifth marriage and our fourth time standing up."

"Oh shit." She laughed. "I had no idea. His marriages mustn't have lasted long."

"No. They didn't. His last marriage to Anna lasted the longest by a year."

"What about your mom?"

"She's on her third marriage. We stood up for her last wedding as well. Consider yourself lucky that your parents have only been married once and are still married." I glanced over at her.

"I do consider myself lucky. I'm not sure how I would feel if they got divorced."

"It's all my brothers, and I know."

"It must have been hard on you guys."

"It was, but we adapted."

The rain started to come down at a steadier pace, and when I looked over at her, I noticed she was gripping the door handle.

"Are you okay?"

"Yeah. Why?"

"You're gripping the door handle as if you're scared to death."

"Okay. Fine. I don't like driving in the rain. Especially rain like this."

"Why?"

"I just don't. It makes me nervous."

"Julia, I promise it's going to be okay. This isn't even that bad. Just relax." I reached over and placed my hand on top of hers. "Tell me how you ended up working for Steven Hart."

"I saved his life."

"What?" I chuckled.

"Jenni and I were at a restaurant having lunch, and Steven was sitting at the table next to us with a friend of his. I could hear his friend asking him if he was okay, and when I looked over, he was sweating profusely. Then suddenly, he fell out of his chair and hit the floor. I jumped up and ran over to him. When I checked his pulse, there wasn't one, so I started CPR and told his friend to call 911. After a few minutes, he came back. Then the paramedics arrived, put him on a stretcher, and I rode with him in the ambulance. His wife was out of town visiting her mother, so I stayed with him at the hospital until she arrived."

"Did he have a heart attack?"

"He did. He couldn't thank me enough for saving him, and when he found out I didn't have a job, he hired me as his personal assistant."

"Why did you leave your position at the coffee shop?"

"I had my reasons."

"It's a good thing you were there," I said.

"Yeah. He called me his guardian angel." Her lips gave way to a small smile.

~

*J*ulia

We'd been driving about two hours in the rain that was moderate and steady. Sam's phone pinged, and when he went to take it from where it sat in the cup holder, I quickly grabbed it from his hand.

"Excuse me?" He glanced at me.

"You need to keep your eyes on the road. Especially in this weather. No looking at your phone."

"Hand me my phone, Julia, so I can see who texted me." His voice was stern.

"No, Sam." I shook my head.

He let out a sigh of irritation.

"Fine. Hold it up to my face to unlock it, and you can tell me who texted me."

I did as he said, and when the phone unlocked, there was a text message from Casey.

"It's from Casey. He said their connecting flight to New York is canceled due to the storms, and they can't get another flight out until tomorrow morning at six a.m."

"Tell him it's okay, stay safe, and I'll see him tomorrow."

I sent the text message and set his phone back in the cupholder. The further we drove, the heavier the rain became, and the windshield wipers automatically sped up, causing a chattering sound as it battled the rain. I gripped the edge of the seat as my nails dug into the fine leather. My heart started racing as the chattering grew intense. The clouds above darkened the sky and made it seem later than it really was. My mind went to that night. The darkness, the pounding of the rain, the chattering of the windshield wipers against the windshield, and the bright lights of the cars that passed us. My heart pounded faster, my skin heated, and the air felt like it was choking the life out of me.

"Stop the car!" I shouted.

"What?" Sam looked over at me. "I can't stop the car, Julia."

"Pull over! Please, Sam." I gasped for air.

"Julia, what is wrong?"

"I can't breathe."

He swerved to the right lane and pulled over on the side

of the road. I quickly pulled the door handle, climbed out of the car, and fell to my knees.

"Julia!" Sam shouted.

I knelt on the ground and lowered my head as my hands planted themselves in the gravel. Sam climbed out and ran over to me. He gripped me from behind and leaned his chin on my shoulder.

"Breathe, Julia."

"I can't." The tears streamed down my face as I struggled to take a breath.

"Yes, you can. Take slow and steady breaths." His grip tightened around me. "Just focus on my voice. You got this. Slow and steady. And as soon as you're ready, we'll get back in the car and wait for the rain to slow down. I won't drive if you don't want me to. I can wait as long as you need me to. Sound like a plan?"

I slowly nodded my head as I could feel the air fill my lungs.

"I'm okay," I said.

"Are you sure?"

"Yes."

He helped me up from the ground, held my face in his hands, and stared into my eyes.

"Can you get back in the car now, or do you need a few minutes?"

"I can get back in the car."

He opened the door, and I climbed inside. After opening the trunk, he climbed into the driver's side and handed me one of his sweatshirts.

"Here. Use this to try and dry off," he said as he turned on the heat.

"Thanks. I'm sorry, Sam."

"Don't be. Did something happen to you during a storm?"

I swallowed hard and slowly nodded my head.

"Can you tell me what?"

"I will when we get to the house." I looked at the navigation screen, and we only had about twenty minutes until we got there. "The rain seems to be lightening up, and we only have twenty more minutes left, so just drive."

"Are you sure?"

"Yes. I really just want to get out of these wet clothes."

"Okay."

He put the car in drive and then reached over and grabbed my hand.

"Lean the seat back, close your eyes and just focus on my hand," he said as he slowly rubbed his thumb back and forth across my skin. "Don't focus on anything else."

Closing my eyes, the feel of his hand against mine soothed me. Just like his grip around me did. I was humiliated, and I owed him my story after what he'd done for me.

# CHAPTER 17

*S*am

      She scared the shit out of me. Nothing scared me, but what I saw her going through did. I held her hand the rest of the way to the house. The rain was steady, but it was only going to get worse as the winds were picking up. She promised to tell me what happened to her once we arrived, but I didn't want to push her. I'd let her tell me when she was ready.

"We're here, Julia."

She let out a deep breath as I climbed out, and I grabbed our bags from the trunk. Opening her door, I helped her out, and we walked up the flight of stairs to the guesthouse. Slipping the key into the lock, I opened the door and flipped the light switch on the left.

"Wow. This is amazing," Julia spoke as she took off her shoes.

"Thank you." I set our bags down.

"You designed this?"

"I did. Right after Casey and Kris bought the house two years ago. They have a lot of family that comes and visits during the summer. You can take the main bedroom, and I'll take the second bedroom. I'm going to change out of these wet clothes. There's a great hydrotherapy tub in the master bath if you want to take a hot bath."

"Thank you. Maybe I'll do that."

I took her bag and set it on the floor in her room. After changing out of my wet clothes, I went over to the bar in the living room and poured myself a scotch. Taking it to the kitchen, I opened the refrigerator that was filled with a fresh fruit tray, vegetable tray, a charcuterie board, cocktail shrimp, guacamole, and two different kinds of lunch meats and cheeses.

"Damn, Casey. You didn't have to do all this," I said out loud.

I pulled out the trays and set them on the counter. I wasn't sure if Julia was hungry or not, but I was.

"What's all this?" Julia asked as she walked into the kitchen wearing a black bathrobe with her hair in a high ponytail. Damn, she looked sexy.

"Compliments of Kris and Casey. Are you feeling better?"

"Yeah. I am." A small smile crossed her face. "That tub is amazing."

"I'm going to make a sandwich. Do you want one?"

"No, thanks. I'm good with all this stuff here."

I found the plates and took two of them down from the cabinet.

"Do you think there are crackers?" she asked.

"Probably. Check the cabinets," I spoke as I grabbed the bread from the counter.

"Ah, ha. We have crackers." She grinned as she pulled out the box.

"There's wine over there in the wine rack if you want to grab a bottle."

"I think I'll have this." She picked up my glass of scotch.

"It's all yours." The corners of my mouth curved upward.

She took a little bit of everything and sat down at the table. Seeing her in that robe and knowing what she had underneath killed me. One time with her wasn't enough. As hard as I tried to convince myself it was, it wasn't. The more time we spent together, the more I wanted her, to be buried inside her, and to feel the warmth of her skin against mine. My cock began to rise, and I needed to stop thinking about it. After making my sandwich, I grabbed some fruit from the fruit tray and joined her at the table.

"Good?" I pointed to her plate.

"Delicious" — she paused for a moment. "Sam, I'm really sorry about earlier. I never wanted you, or anyone, for that matter, to see me like that."

"You have nothing to be sorry for, Julia."

As I stared into her eyes, I saw the tears rise and the despair that overtook them.

"What happened to you?" I asked in a soft voice.

"My boyfriend and I were in a serious car accident four years ago during a storm. I lived, and he didn't."

"Julia, I'm so sorry."

"He had the whole night planned out, but he wouldn't tell me where we were going. He said he wanted it to be a surprise. As we were driving, the rain came out of nowhere. It hit the windshield so hard that he couldn't see. A semi-truck was coming around a curve at a high speed, crossed the line, and hit us so hard that the car rolled four times before a tree stopped it. Everything happened so fast, but I still remember counting the number of rolls. It took me a minute to process what had happened, and I could feel something dripping down my face. When I brought my hand up to feel it, it was covered in blood. I looked over at Justin, and he was unconscious. I reached my hand over, began shaking him, and screamed at him to wake up. When I felt his pulse, it was weak. When I tried to open the door, it wouldn't budge. I'd never felt so trapped in my life. Then I started drifting in and out of consciousness until I heard Justin's voice. All he said was, 'wake up, Julia. You must wake up. It's time to wake up and move on with your life.' Then suddenly, my eyes opened, and I was in the hospital. My parents told me that I had a brain bleed, and the doctors rushed me into emergency surgery. They put me in a medically induced coma for two weeks, and when they reversed it, I wouldn't wake up—until I heard Justin's voice. I remember asking for him, and that's when my parents told me he had died before the paramedics got to us. A few days later, when I was more coherent, my sister handed me a small ring box and told me he had it in his coat pocket because he was going to ask me to marry him that night." She wiped her eyes. "So, yeah. That's why I freak out and won't get in a car when it storms."

I reached across the table and grabbed her hand. "Why didn't you tell me earlier? I never would have made you get in that car. My God, Julia. I am so sorry. You tried to tell me, and I just dismissed it."

"You had no idea, and I thought I could handle it. I wanted to be able to handle it. But then it all came flooding back, and I freaked out."

"I'm really sorry about Justin. I can't even imagine."

"A few weeks later, I went back to work at the coffee shop. But the memories there were too painful. Every day, Justin would walk through the door at one o'clock on his lunch break to see me and get a cup of coffee. And every day after, I watched the door and waited for him to walk through it even though I knew he wouldn't. So, I quit. And a couple of months later is when I met Steven."

"Did he know what you had been through?"

"Yeah. I told him because I would sometimes burst into

tears at the most random times. He and his wife set me up with a really good therapist friend of theirs."

"Did the therapy help?"

"Yeah. It did. It took a while, but it helped. Tomorrow is the anniversary of his death."

"I never should have made you come." I slowly shook my head.

"No. If I didn't want to, I would have told you. And my dad agreed that it would be good for me to get away from California for a couple of days."

"Do you still feel that way considering—"

"Yeah. I do. I wish my sister were here. We have this thing we do when one of us is feeling down."

"What do you do?"

"You'll see." The corners of her mouth curved upward as she got up from the table and poured herself a glass of wine. "Alexa, play Cry to Me by Solomon Burke."

I smiled as the song began to play, and she started dancing around the kitchen with the wine glass in her hand. I got up from my chair and danced around with her. Grabbing her hand, I twirled her around and then pulled her into me and my arms locked securely around her from behind. Bringing her arm up, she placed her hand on the back of my head as we swayed back and forth to the melody. Closing my eyes, I took in her scent. A clean, soft natural scent that drove me mad with desire. The song ended, and I didn't want to let her go. So, I didn't.

"All I want at this moment is you," I whispered in her ear.

# CHAPTER 18

*J*ulia

My skin trembled at his touch. The warmth of his breath against my flesh made my belly flutter, and his words sent shivers down my spine. The hardness of his cock pressed against my lower back, and I wanted him as much as he wanted me. I needed him because I needed to escape the pain I felt inside. My fingers softly moved back and forth across the back of his head as his hands untied the strings of my robe, and he slid it off my body. His scent took me in. A fine gentleman's cologne that was masculine, crisp, and clean with a hint of spice. His hands roamed up and down the silk fabric of my black nightie. One hand stayed planted on my breast while the other one traveled down until his fingers met the edge of my panties. Pushing them to the side, his finger circled me before it dipped inside. A gasp escaped me as his hand moved from my breast up to my neck. Tilting my head back, his lips met mine. His finger moved in and out of me while his thumb pressed against my clit. I was paralyzed with pleasure and couldn't wait for the explosion that was on its way. The orgasm took over me, and the sounds that escaped me told him I was satisfied, at least for now.

Turning around, I got down on my knees and undid his pants, for I wanted him in every way. Sliding off his pants and briefs, I stroked his hard cock with my hand before shoving it in my mouth. A roar erupted in his chest and his fingers tangled in my hair. I took him in, and I took him in deep. I wanted to devour every inch of him.

"My God, you're amazing. But I need you to stop before I come."

He picked me up in his arms and carried me upstairs to the bedroom. After lying me down, he removed my nightie, tossed it over the bed, and wasted no time taking my hardened peaks in his mouth. The fire below erupted and was begging to be fanned.

"I need to get a condom from my wallet," he softly spoke as his finger ran down my cheek.

"Don't ruin this moment. I'm on birth control, and as long as you're clea—"

"I am clean. I take that very seriously."

"Then we don't need a condom," I whispered.

The corners of his mouth curved upward as he thrust inside, burying himself as far as he could. After a lot of movement, he rolled on his back and pulled me on top of him. I rode him hard and fast until I came. His hands gripped my hips, and he held me down while he exploded inside me. My body collapsed on top of his as my rapid breathing began to slow, and his arms tightened around me.

"Fuck, Julia," he spoke with bated breath, and I let out a tiny laugh.

I lifted my head, and our eyes locked. Bringing his hand up to my cheek, his thumb swept across my lips while the corners of his mouth curved upward.

"What?" I smirked.

"Nothing. How about I go get us a glass of wine."

"I'd like that."

I climbed off him and walked to the bathroom. When I was finished, I picked my nightie up off the floor, slipped into it, and went downstairs to get my phone from my purse. When I walked into the kitchen, I saw Sam cleaning up.

"This can wait until the morning," I said.

"Uh, no, it can't."

"That's right. You're OCD."

"I am not." He turned and looked at me.

"Sure, you are." A smile crossed my lips as I helped him.

"Why do you say that?"

"Because your house is spotless. Too clean for a bachelor. Plus, you have mad closet organizational skills."

He set the plate down on the counter and cocked his head.

"When did you see my closet?" His eye steadily narrowed at me.

"When I went to your house to get your wallet."

"You went in my closet?" His brow arched.

"I did, and to be honest, I'm kind of sorry I did. I can't unsee what I saw."

"What do you mean?"

"The way your clothes and shoes are organized by designer, color, etc. It's freaky."

"There is nothing freaky about being organized." He pointed at me.

"Are your brothers the same way?"

"No. They're not."

"Admit that you were cringing when you came to my apartment and saw the dishes in the sink." I smiled.

"I didn't notice."

"Yes, you did!" I laughed. "I saw you glance over there."

"Answer me this, Miss Benton. Why is it so hard to open

the dishwasher that is right next to the sink and put your dishes in when you're done with them?"

He had a point, and I didn't have an answer. So, I just shrugged.

"I'll let you know when I figure it out."

When we finished cleaning up, and Sam made sure the kitchen was sparkling clean, he poured us a glass of wine, and we went upstairs.

"Tell me about Sam Kind," I said as I sat with my legs crossed on the bed facing him.

"What do you want to know?"

"Anything."

"You already know about my parents and their marriages, and you know I have three brothers. I graduated from the University of California with a master's in Architecture and Engineering and went to work for my father."

"Have you always wanted to be an architect?"

"I have. Ever since I was a kid. I love to create things, and I love to solve problems."

"Hmm. So do your brothers, right? Stefan loves to build things, so he has a passion for creating. Sebastian loves to create new foods and dishes, Simon loves solving problems, and he's good. That's why he's a detective."

"Very good." He smiled. "I'm sure being a twin, you and your sister have a lot of the same qualities."

"There is one difference between us. She's more of a partier, and I like a quieter scene. But I'm not opposed to a great party every now and again."

"Cheers to that." He smiled as he held his glass up to me, and I tapped mine against it.

"Thank you," I said as I placed my hand on his leg.

"For what?"

"For being so understanding and helping me get through this weekend. You'd think after four years, I'd be over it."

"You loved him. I would imagine that is something you'd never get over. Tell me about him."

"Really?" My brows furrowed.

"Yes. He must have been someone pretty special to have someone like you."

"He was really sweet. And nice. Everyone loved him. There wasn't one person that didn't like him. He'd go out of his way to help anyone in need. Even if he had only one dollar to his name, he would give it to someone who needed it. He would do anything for me."

"How long were the two of you together?"

"We had been together three years before the accident. He had just moved to Los Angeles from Seattle for work. He was in advertising and his company transferred him to their new offices. His car broke down, his phone was dead, and he came into the coffee shop to see if he could use someone's phone to call a tow truck. I let him use mine, and we talked while he waited for the tow truck to come." I could feel the tears spring to my eyes.

Sam reached over and placed his hand on mine.

"I'm sorry," he spoke in a mere whisper.

"It's fine. Sometimes I sit and think how different my life would be right now if he were still alive. Do you ever think of things like that? I mean, do you ever think that if one little thing never would have happened, your life would be completely different."

"Yeah. Sometimes I do."

"Anyway, why hasn't some crazy hot chick snatched you up yet?" I grinned before finishing off my wine.

"Trust me. They've tried. But I really don't believe or have too much faith in relationships. A perfect example are my parents."

"I guess I could understand that."

"Have you dated anyone since Justin?"

"Nah. I just like having one-night stands." A smirk crossed my lips. "The thought of losing someone again just isn't appealing to me. My therapist told me that I have what's called 'fear of loss' and that I'm stuck in the hole of avoidance. Which isn't healthy, by the way." I pointed at him, and he chuckled. "But it's my hole, and if I want to stay in it, I will for as long as I want to."

"And what does your family say?"

"My sister understands. She can feel me and my emotions. You would understand that seeing you're a quadruplet."

"I do." He nodded his head.

"My mom pressures me to start dating again, but my dad tells her to stop and leave me alone. Do your brothers feel the same way about relationships as you do?"

"Yes. None of us are looking to commit to anyone."

I let out a long yawn.

"Why don't we get some sleep?" he said.

"Good idea. Since you're already comfy in the bed, you might as well just stay. There's no sense in messing up two beds."

"I like the way you think." The corners of his mouth curved upward.

I got up from the bed, and when I went to set my empty glass on the nightstand, he stopped me.

"I'll take that." He held out his hand.

"You're seriously going to take the glasses downstairs, right now?" My brow arched.

"Yeah. I am."

"We can bring them down in the morning."

"No. They need to be taken downstairs and washed before we go to bed."

"If you say so." I handed him my glass.

"Why wake up to a mess. It just starts the day off on a bad note," he said.

I stared at him with a narrowed eye.

"I bet you're one of those who makes the bed the second you get up."

"Damn right I do. You don't?"

"Eventually, I do. But not the second I climb out of bed."

"You should." He pointed his finger at me as a smirk crossed his face.

"And you should drink your coffee black."

"Never." He winked before walking out of the bedroom.

# CHAPTER 19

*S*am

After washing the wine glasses and putting them away, I headed back upstairs to bed. When I walked into the room, Julia was already sound asleep. Climbing in, I stared at her for a few moments while she slept. I had no idea that she'd been through so much trauma, and I felt for her. Seeing her from the outside, you'd never know she'd lost the man she loved so much to a tragic accident. She was always so happy. But inside, she was shattered—a shattered woman who was too afraid to love anyone ever again. I felt incredibly sorry for her. But I liked that she felt that way because I didn't have anything to worry about with her. Perhaps we could continue carrying on a sexual relationship. Why not? She was incredibly sexy, a goddess between the sheets, and the only thing she wanted was sex. It felt like we were two peas in a pod. We both wanted the same thing without any emotional attachment. We'd have to keep it under wraps because she was my personal assistant. If Grayson or my father found out, I'd be dead.

The next morning, I opened my eyes, and she wasn't next

to me. Looking at the clock, it was seven a.m., and I could hear music coming from downstairs. Pulling on a pair of sweatpants, and after making the bed, I followed the music into the kitchen and saw Julia holding her phone, dancing around and singing to the song Spirit in the Sky. I crossed my arms as I leaned against the wall and watched her.

"Oh my God, you scared me," she said when she saw me.

"Go on. Keep doing what you're doing." I smirked.

When the song ended, I lightly clapped.

"Say hi to Jenni." She smiled as she held up the phone to me.

"Hi, Jenni."

"Hey, Sam. Thanks for taking care of my sister this weekend. It really means a lot to me."

"You're welcome." I smiled at her.

"Thanks for the dance, Jenni, but I should go."

"Yeah. Me too. Enjoy the rest of your time in New York. I'll talk to you tomorrow. I love you, dork."

"I love you too, dork."

After ending the call, Julia turned and looked at me.

"I'm sorry if I woke you."

"No. You didn't wake me. So, what was all that about?" I asked as I popped a K-cup in the Keurig.

"Jenni called, and we thought it would be a good idea to dance—cause, you know."

"Yeah. I know. Isn't that song a little morbid? I'm sorry. I shouldn't have said—"

"You don't have to keep saying you're sorry, Sam, but thank you. And that was one of his favorite songs."

As soon as the coffee was done brewing, I walked over to the refrigerator and looked for the cream.

"Seriously? There's no cream or milk?" I turned and looked at her as she sat there with a smirk on her face.

"I guess not."

"Did you hide it?"

"No." She let out a laugh. "I honestly don't think there is any."

"Now, what the hell am I supposed to do?"

She walked over, picked up my cup, and held it up to me.

"Cross over to the dark side, young Skywalker."

"Very funny." I tapped her nose. "There's a coffee place about a mile up the road. I'll get dressed and go. Do you want anything?"

"No." She let out a sigh. "You made the bed already, didn't you?"

"Maybe. Why?"

"Just wondering." She took her coffee and sat down at the table.

~

*W*hile I was waiting for my coffee, my phone rang, and Casey was calling.

"Hey, Case."

"Sam, I'm sorry, man. Our flight is delayed again. We boarded the plane this morning and sat there forever until they made us get off due to a mechanical issue with the plane. Now we have to wait for them to bring in another plane and they don't know how long it's going to be. Kris and I talked about it, and we're just going to stay in Los Angeles until Monday. Is there any way we can meet up when you get back tomorrow?"

"Yeah. Of course. Just shoot me a text and tell me what you're thinking about doing, and I'll draw something up. We can discuss it tomorrow."

"Sounds good. I'm sorry."

"Don't be. Shit happens."

"I feel bad I made you come out there, and I can't even get home."

"It's fine. It feels good to get out of Los Angeles for a couple of days."

~

*J*ulia

While Sam was out getting coffee, I took my cup and walked out to the lake. This place was not only beautiful, but it was also a sea of tranquility. Sitting down in one of the white Adirondack chairs, I held the warm cup between my hands and stared out at the peacefulness of the water while I took in the cool, crisp morning air.

"Hey," Sam spoke as he walked up. "What are you doing?"

"Just enjoying the peacefulness of the lake. Are you happy now?" I smirked as I pointed to his coffee cup.

"Very." He smiled as he held up his cup. "Casey called me, and they're still stuck in Los Angeles. Apparently, there's a mechanical issue with the plane, and they've been delayed again. So, he and Kris decided to stay in Los Angeles until Monday. We're going to meet up tomorrow when we get back. I'm going to walk around and check out the property, take some pictures, and draw something up quick just to give him an idea. Care to join me?"

"Sure. I'd love to."

He held out his hand and helped me up from my chair. After walking around and snapping some pictures, we headed back to the house and enjoyed a bagel he'd brought back with him.

"I need to take a shower, and then we can head out," he said.

"Me too. You can take a shower in the master bath, and I'll use the one in the other bathroom."

"Or maybe we can just take one together." The corners of his mouth curved upward.

"Let's go." I grinned.

# CHAPTER 20

*S*am

On the plane ride home, I opened my laptop and finished the design for Casey's house expansion. Julia and I spent the latter part of yesterday and evening in the city. We checked out the building I wanted to see, walked around and explored a bit of the city, enjoyed a great dinner, and then went back to the suite and had fantastic sex. It was a trip I wouldn't forget about anytime soon.

After we landed back in Los Angeles, I drove her home. Grabbing her bag from the car, I walked her up to her apartment.

"Thanks, Sam. I had a really good time."

"You're welcome." I set her bag down. "Listen, Julia. We need to discuss something."

"I already know." She smiled. "Nobody can know what happened between us on our trip."

"Yeah. It has to be our little secret."

"Don't worry. I'm good at keeping secrets." Her lips gave way to a smirk.

"Okay. I should go. I need to call Casey and let him know I'm back."

I brought my hand up to her cheek and softly stroked it.

"I'll see you tomorrow morning," I said.

"See you tomorrow."

I walked out of her apartment and headed home. When I got there, I saw Stefan and Lily down by the beach.

"Welcome home, brother. How was New York?"

"It was good."

"Hi, Uncle Sam." Lily waved.

"Hi, Lily." I gave her a wave back.

"You're back!" I heard Sebastian's voice from behind as he patted my back. "How was your trip?"

"It was great."

"And Julia?" he asked.

"Julia is good. Listen, I have to get back up to the house. Casey and Kris are on their way over."

"Wait. What?" Stefan said. "How are they here when you just saw them in New York?"

"They never made it back to New York. It's a long story. If you guys aren't doing anything later, let's barbeque some steaks, and I'll tell you all about it over a couple of beers."

"Sounds good. We'll do it at my house," Stefan said.

"I'm heading to the restaurant, but I'll leave early. And I'll bring and grill the steaks." Sebastian smirked.

"Are you saying I can't grill steaks?" Stefan punched Sebastian's arm.

"Actually, I am." He playfully punched him back.

"I'll text Simon and see what he's doing." I laughed as I shook my head.

Walking up to the house, I sent my brother a text message.

*"Stefan's house tonight for steak and beer. Seven o'clock."*

*"Count me in, bro."*

I printed the design and set it on the table for when Casey and Kris arrived. They both loved it and only made a couple of changes.

"I'll make the changes and have the final copy sent out to you."

"Thanks, Sam." Kris gave me a hug.

"Yeah, man. Thanks. Again, I'm sorry for this weekend."

"Not your fault, Case. It was great seeing you two. Do you have a contractor lined up?"

"We do."

"If there are any problems, let me know."

∼

*I* didn't want to talk in front of Lily, so Stefan sent her to her room to finish her homework after we ate.

"We already know you slept with Julia on your trip, so spill it, Sam," Stefan said.

"No, I didn't."

"You're a fucking liar." Simon grinned as he pointed at me.

"Fine. We had a lot of sex."

"So, come tomorrow morning, you'll no longer have an assistant?" Stefan's brow raised.

"Julia isn't going anywhere, and we're keeping what happened on the down low. She knows nobody can find out."

I opened the refrigerator and pulled out four beers. We took them outside and sat down on the deck in front of the fire pit.

"I found out a lot about her."

"Like?" Sebastian asked.

"Four years ago, she was in a serious car accident with her boyfriend. He died, and she survived. They had to rush her into emergency surgery because her brain was bleeding. She spent some time in a medically induced coma, and when she woke up, she found out he was going to propose to her that night."

"Man, that's awful," Stefan spoke.

"It happened during a storm. It was storming when we were driving to Montauk, and she had a full-on panic attack. She made me pull over, and she got out of the car."

"The storm was a trigger for her," Simon said.

"Yeah. It was bad. Honestly, it scared the hell out of me."

"What did you do?" Sebastian asked.

"I got out of the car, calmed her down, and then we finished the drive to Casey's house."

"And?" Simon asked.

"We spent the night talking and having sex. And again, the next night. And this morning before we left for the airport." I smiled.

"Sounds to me like someone may have caught some feelings." Sebastian smirked.

"No. It's not like that."

"I was referring to her, Sam."

"Nah, man. She isn't looking for a relationship. She's too afraid of loss."

"She told you that?" Stefan asked.

"Yeah. That's the reason she hasn't dated since Justin. She just has one-night stands here and there."

"So basically, she's an 'us.'" A smirk crossed Simon's lips.

"Yeah. Which is perfect because I don't have to worry about anything with her."

"You're going to keep screwing her, aren't you?" Stefan asked.

"Hopefully." I grinned.

"I can see a disaster on the horizon," Sebastian spoke. "There's no way the two of you can keep doing the dirty deed and someone not catch some feelings. And maybe it won't be her."

"Shut up. You know better than that."

My phone pinged in my pocket, and when I pulled it out, I had a text message from Julia.

*"Hi. What did Casey and his wife think about the design?"*

"I bet that's from Julia. She's missing your ass right now." Stefan laughed.

"Actually, it is from her. She just wants to know how Casey liked the design."

"She couldn't wait to ask you in the morning?" Sebastian asked.

*"Hi. Overall, they loved it and only made a couple of changes."*

*"That's great."*

*"What are you doing?"* I asked her.

*"I just got home from my parents' house. I'm going to take a hot bath and get ready for bed. You?"*

*"Sitting around a fire pit with my brothers. But I'm ready to head home as well. Sleep tight, and I'll see you in the morning."*

*"You too, Sam."*

"That's some serious text messaging going on," Stefan spoke.

"Shut the fuck up." I threw a bottle cap at him. "Anyway, I'm going home. I still have to unpack, and I'm tired."

"I'm sure all that sex wore you out." Sebastian chuckled

"Damn. You are all nothing but a bunch of jealous whores." I grinned as I stood up from my seat. "I'll see you tomorrow."

~

*S*tefan
The three of us sat there and watched our brother walk back to his house.

"Do you two feel what I feel?" I asked.

"Yeah. I feel it," Simon said.

"Me too," Sebastian spoke.

"He's falling for her," I said.

"Even though he's trying to hide it from us, it's obvious," my brother Simon said.

"Totally obvious." Sebastian sighed.

"What do we do?" I asked.

"What can we do?" Simon said. "We'll just have to sit back and watch how this unfolds."

"One of them is going to get hurt," Sebastian said.

"Somehow, I don't think it'll be Sam." I sighed.

# CHAPTER 21

## ONE WEEK LATER

*J*ulia

I didn't tell my parents about the panic attack I had in New York. There was no point in worrying them. Plus, my mom would talk about it for the next couple of months. My sister and I both agreed a long time ago that some things were better left unsaid where our parents were concerned.

Sam and I spent a couple of nights together during the week, and my sister called to tell me that her photoshoot ended early, and she'd be coming home within the next week.

"Hello, Julia," Sam's dad said as he walked up to my desk.

"Good morning, Mr. Kind."

"I wanted to give you this in person." He handed me an envelope. "It's an invitation to my wedding next week. I know it's short notice, but now that you're working for us, I would love for you to attend."

"Thank you. I'd love to celebrate your wedding."

"Excellent. We look forward to having you. Where's Sam?"

"He had to meet with a client first thing this morning."

"How are things working out for you here?"

"Great. I couldn't be happier." I smiled.

"There aren't any issues or anything?"

"Nope. Everything is good."

"Glad to hear that. When Sam gets in, send him to my office."

"I will. Thanks again for the invitation." I smiled brightly.

"You're welcome, sweetheart." He tapped the edge of my desk.

As I was in Sam's office setting a typed-up contract on his desk, he walked in.

"You look nice," he spoke.

Turning around, my eyes locked with his.

"New suit?" I asked.

"Actually, it is. What do you think?"

"It looks great on you. Did you already secure a special place next to the other dark gray suits you own?"

"Very funny. If you weren't so cute, I'd slap you."

"Maybe that's what I was going for." The corners of my mouth curved upward.

"You're bad, Miss Benton. Plans tonight?"

"Are you asking me out?"

"Maybe." He smirked.

"Then I'm free."

"Good."

"Your dad wants to see you."

"Did he say what it's about?"

"No. He gave me an invitation to his wedding."

"That's great. Are you going?"

"Yeah. It'll be fun." I grinned.

"Then I'll send a car to pick you up. Book us a room at the hotel. I want to drink freely without any worry about driving home."

"Aren't you afraid someone will see us?"

"No. We'll be careful." He gave me a wink.

"I'll go book it now." I turned on my heels and walked out of his office.

~

## Sam

"You wanted to see me, Dad?" I asked as I saw Stefan sitting across from him.

"Yes, son. Come in and shut the door. Have a seat." He gestured. "I've been thinking about something for quite a while. When Celeste and I get back from our honeymoon, I'm going to retire and leave the company in both your hands.

"Retire? Already?" Stefan asked.

"Boys, it's time. I want to travel with Celeste, and I can't do that and worry about the company. We talked about it, and she agreed with me. It's time you two step up and take over."

"Wow, Dad. I don't know what to say," I said.

"We'll discuss the details after the wedding. But I do intend to be done within a few months."

"Thanks, Dad. You've worked hard for this, and you deserve it," Stefan said.

"Thanks, son. Now, if you'll excuse me, I have a meeting with my lawyer."

Stefan and I walked out of his office and high-fived each other.

"Yes!" he exclaimed.

"It's about time." I chuckled.

"Let's celebrate tonight," Stefan said.

"As much as I'd love to, I made plans with Julia already."

"She'll understand if you cancel. This is big. I'll call Simon and Sebastian, and the four of us will hit the town."

"I'm not canceling on Julia. We'll do it another night."

"Wow. This is a first." His brows furrowed.

"Why are you making a big deal about it?"

"Why are you choosing her over us?" He followed me into my office and shut the door.

"I'm not choosing anyone over anyone. I already made plans with her for tonight. That would be very rude to cancel them."

"Ha. Since when the fuck do you care about being rude? Especially where a chick is concerned. You're falling for her." He pointed at me.

"No. I'm not! Friday night would be better because then we can party all night without worrying about stumbling into the office the next morning with a massive hangover. Agree?"

He stood there and stared at me for a moment.

"Fine. I'll let Sebastian and Simon know. But you know Sebastian usually works Friday nights."

"He can skip this Friday," I said. "It's his restaurant, and he can do whatever he wants."

"Whatever, bro." He shook his head and walked out of my office.

∼

*J* thought it would be better for me to stay at Julia's tonight because I didn't want to hear shit from my brothers if they saw her. Knocking on her door, she answered with a bright smile. A smile that always made me happy regardless of whether I was in a bad mood.

"Hi."

"Hi," I said as I stepped inside.

"I figured I would cook for you tonight."

"It smells delicious in here. What are you making?"

"Chicken parmesan. I hope you like that. It's my mom's award-winning recipe."

"I love chicken parmesan."

"I'm happy to hear that because I was worried."

I followed her to the kitchen and nearly stopped breathing when I saw the mess.

"Maybe it's best if you don't look in here."

"Do you not clean up as you cook?"

"I try." She scrunched her nose at me.

"Let me help you."

"No, no." She placed her hand on my chest. "You're my guest. I'll clean it up later."

"It's not up for discussion." I rolled up my sleeves. "And I'm not your guest, I'm your boss, and you have to do as I say."

"It's after work hours, Sam."

"Have you forgotten that your job as my personal assistant is 24/7? There are no set work hours."

"Right." She bit down on her bottom lip.

"You just keep doing what you were doing, and I'll get some of this mess cleaned up."

"Okay. I just have to make the salad."

"You go ahead and do that." I smiled at her.

I started with the mess in the sink. Opening her dishwasher, I noticed it was full of dishes.

"Oh. Those are clean. I haven't had a chance to unload it."

I took in a deep breath and washed the dirty dishes by hand. By the time I washed, dried, and put them away, it was time to eat.

"You really didn't have to do that," she said as she poured some wine into our glasses.

"Yes. Yes, I did. Next time, you should try cleaning up as

you're cooking. It makes a world of difference and saves time at the end of the meal when you have to clean up the rest."

"I will keep that in mind, Mr. Clean. Thank you." A smirk crossed her beautiful face.

"'Mr. Clean?' Really?" I got up from my chair.

She quickly stood up and started walking backwards with her hands up.

"It's a very fitting name for you. I could call you worse." She grinned as she turned to make a run for it.

I was quicker and wrapped one arm around her waist from behind and held her in my grip.

"Where do you think you're going?" I spoke in her ear in an authoritative tone.

"I was heading to the kitchen since you cleaned the counter and all."

I loosened my grip, and the moment she turned around in my arms, my mouth smashed into hers. My fingers curled around the bottom of her shirt as I pulled it over her head and tossed it on the floor. While I unbuttoned my shirt, she took down her pants and revealed the sexiest panties I'd ever seen. Picking her up, she wrapped her legs around me as I carried her over to the kitchen and set her on the counter. Our lips tangled, and our tongues met with pleasure as I unhooked her bra. Sliding my tongue across her soft neck, I made my way down to her supple breasts and took her hardened peaks in my mouth. I didn't think I could get any harder than I already was, but I did. Gripping the sides of her panties, I slid them off and tossed them to the ground. Her legs around my waist tightened as I brought her to the edge of the counter and thrust inside her. Moans escaped our lips as pleasure and intoxication soared through us.

"Is this what you wanted?" I rapidly thrust in and out of her.

"Yes," she spoke with bated breath. "Oh my God, yes!"

Her legs were vice grips around my waist as her body released an orgasm, causing me to explode inside her at the same time. I slowed my thrusts and strained to give her every drop I had inside me.

My heart rate was erratic as I stayed buried inside her, unable to move. Staring into her eyes, I swallowed hard at the feeling that washed over me.

"What's wrong?" she asked as her arms stayed wrapped around my neck.

"Nothing. Absolutely, nothing." I smiled as I kissed her lips.

After pulling out of her, I helped her down from the counter.

"The bleach is under the sink," she said as she walked away. "I know you're dying to use it. And by the way, don't tell my sister we fucked on the counter. It's a rule we have here." She smirked as she walked down the hallway towards her bedroom.

# CHAPTER 22

## ONE WEEK LATER

*S*am
 The four of us took our place next to our dad and waited for the ceremony to start. This wedding ceremony took place in the Crystal Gardens at the Beverly Hills Hotel, followed by an elegant black-tie reception in the Crystal Ballroom.

"This better be the last time I'm standing up here," Sebastian whispered in my ear.

"No shit. Enough is enough already."

I had my head turned talking to Simon when Sebastian smacked my chest with the back of his hand.

"D-A-M-N!"

Turning my head, I nearly lost my breath when I saw Julia walking down the white runner. Her lips formed a smile as her hand gave a small wave while she sat next to Grayson.

"Wow. She looks incredible," Stefan said.

"All three of you keep your eyes to yourself and off my personal assistant."

"Sorry, bro," Simon spoke up. "That's kind of hard to do."

I agreed with him because she was the most beautiful

woman in the place. She wore a long black sleeveless gown with a plunging neckline and a slit that went too far up her leg. Her hair was pinned up with a few curls around her face, and her lips were painted cherry red. I placed my hand in my pocket to keep my throbbing cock under control.

After the ceremony ended, we stayed back while all the guests headed to the ballroom to take an obscene number of pictures.

"I just want to get to drinking," Sebastian said. "These pictures with us are a waste of our time because they're going to end up in the trash when they get divorced."

"Right?" Stefan laughed.

"What's so funny, Daddy?" Lily asked as she looked up at him.

"Nothing, baby. Smile for the camera."

"It's kind of nice to have the one with just the four of us," I said. "We can compare this one with the other three we have and see how much we've changed."

"You're a dork," Simon playfully punched me.

Finally, we were finished except for Stefan, who had to stay back and have photos taken of just him and Lily. We headed to the Crystal Ballroom, and I grabbed a glass of champagne from the waiter as he walked by. I looked around for Julia and saw her standing and talking to Grayson and Joan.

"Hi." I smiled. "Can I talk to you in private for a moment?"

"Sure." She grinned.

I led her over to a quiet corner where nobody else was.

"You look absolutely stunning."

"Thank you. You look very handsome in that tuxedo, Mr. Kind. All four of you do."

"Thanks."

"The ceremony was beautiful," she said.

"It was okay. Same as all the others." I gave her a smirk. "Did you take your bag up to the room?"

"I did. In fact, I got ready for the wedding there. Grayson saw me in the hallway. Apparently, his room is two down from ours."

"Shit. What did he say?"

"He just asked if I was staying here, and I told him I was so I didn't have to worry about driving home."

"Good girl. I wouldn't put it past him to check with the staff to see if I got a room here. Good thinking about putting it in your name."

"Julia!" Lily came running over.

"Hey there, Lily." She smiled brightly as she knelt in front of her. "You look like a princess."

"So do you. Did you see the ice sculpture of the two connecting hearts?"

"I don't think I did."

"Come with me." Lily grinned as she took hold of Julia's hand.

My brothers walked up, and Sebastian put his hand on my back.

"You're falling for her. If you haven't already."

"Funny. That's what I tell him every day," Stefan said.

"All of you knock it off. I am not. We have a good uncomplicated work/sexual relationship. That's all."

"We see the way you look at her, bro," Simon said.

"Yeah. And if we even dare try to look at her that way, you rip our heads off," Stefan said.

"That's because she's my personal assistant. If it were any other woman, I'd tell you to go for it. But not with someone that works for me. You know the rules."

After dinner, my father and Celeste shared their first dance as husband and wife. Halfway through the song, the announcer told everyone to grab their partner and join them on the dance floor. Stefan grabbed Lily, and I walked over to where Julia stood and held out my hand.

"May I have this dance?"

"Of course." She smiled, and Grayson narrowed his eye at me.

"Should we be doing this?"

"It's a wedding. A lot of people dance. There's nothing wrong with me dancing with my personal assistant."

"Hi, Uncle Sam." Lily smiled as she and Stefan danced over to us. "Can we switch? I want to dance with you."

I looked at Stefan, who had a broad smile splayed across his face.

"Of course, we can," Julia said. "How sweet is that."

I let go of Julia and danced with Lily. How could I say no to her? But I was sure Stefan had something to do with it.

The song ended, and immediately another song came on. Sebastian stepped in between Stefan and Julia, took her hand, and began to dance. I inhaled a sharp breath as I stood over to the side and watched them. Halfway through the song, Simon stepped in and took his turn.

"I hate all of you," I said as Stefan and Sebastian stood next to me. "What the fuck is wrong with you?"

They started laughing, and I needed another drink.

～

*J*ulia

His hand held my arms above my head, and his body hovered over me while his thrusting became rapid, and his lips tangled with mine. My body was at the edge of the cliff and getting ready to dive into the oblivion of another orgasm. I moaned as my legs tightened around him. His thrusts became faster while sexy groans rumbled in his chest. With one last thrust, he halted and filled my body with his pleasure.

The corners of my mouth curved upward as he hovered over me, out of breath, and his eyes gazed into mine. He let go of my arms and slowly lowered his body on top of me. Bringing my arms around him, I softly stroked his back while we both waited for our bodies to calm down.

"Okay. Time to get up." I hastily pushed him off me and ran to the bathroom.

"Well, that's a first," he spoke as he walked into the bathroom and covered my naked body with a blanket while I hugged the porcelain god.

He held my hair back from behind until I was done vomiting.

"I'm so sorry," I said.

"Should I take offense?" A sexy smirk crossed his lips.

"It's your fault." I wiped my mouth and leaned my back against the tub. "You kept feeding me all that champagne, and then you were flipping me every which way."

"You didn't enjoy it?" His brow arched. "Because judging by the number of orgasms I gave you—"

"Of course, I enjoyed it. But I don't think the alcohol did."

"Next time you drink too much, I'll be more mindful not to flip you so much." He gave me a wink, and I couldn't help but smile.

"I appreciate your kindness."

He helped me up from the floor, and we both climbed into bed.

"It was a beautiful wedding, though," I said as his arm hooked around me, and I rested my head on his chest.

"They always are." He let out a sigh.

I closed my eyes, and as I lay there snuggled tightly against him, I could feel the tears starting to emerge. Sam Kind had become more to me than just a boss/casual sex partner. He broke through the hard shell I'd built around me the day Justin died. He made me feel again. And for the first time in four years, I saw a possible future with him. I just needed to get him to see that a relationship with me would be a beautiful thing for both of us.

# CHAPTER 23

*S* am
   We both were woken up by the obnoxious knocking on the hotel door.

"What the fuck," I said as I climbed out of bed, pulled on my pants from last night, and walked to the living area of the suite to open it.

"Surprise. Room service has arrived!" Sebastian said as he and my other brothers wheeled a cart inside.

"What the hell are you guys doing?"

"We thought we'd all have breakfast together before we checked out."

"Yummy. I'm starving." Julia smiled as she walked out wearing the hotel-provided robe.

"Good morning, Julia," all three of my brothers spoke at the same time.

"You're looking lovely this morning." Stefan grinned, and I smacked his chest.

"Thank you. What do we have?" she asked as she lifted the silver lids off the plates.

"A little bit of everything," Simon said as he pulled out

one of the chairs at the table that sat eight people. "Have a seat."

"Thank you. I hope there's coffee because I'm seriously hungover, and I need some."

"Your coffee, madame." Sebastian smiled as he set the cup down in front of her. "Cream?"

"Oh god, no."

"Rea—"

"Don't engage, Sebastian," I said as I put my hand up and stopped him.

She rolled her eyes at me and put some scrambled eggs on her plate.

"Simon, are you working tonight?" Sebastian asked.

"No. I'm off this weekend. Why?"

"Stefan? Are you picking Lily up, or is Mom keeping her all weekend?"

"Mom's keeping her until tomorrow. Why?"

"I was thinking you guys could come over, and we'd have a bonfire and kick back a few beers. Sam?"

"Sure. Why not."

"Count me in," Simon said.

"Me too," Stefan spoke.

"Julia, I'd love for you to join us."

"Really?" She grinned.

"Yes."

"I'd love to if it's okay with Sam." She glanced at me.

"I'd like for you to come. Then you can stay the night at my house."

"Okay. But I do have to get up and be out early. My sister is coming home tomorrow."

"That's right. You must be very happy."

"I am. I've missed her so much."

After breakfast, the five of us grabbed our bags and went down to the lobby. When the elevator stopped one floor down and the door opened, the boy's father and Celeste stood there.

"Boys. Julia." My father narrowed his eye at me. "You all got rooms here last night?" he asked as he and his new bride stepped inside.

"Yeah, Dad," Stefan said. "The four of us shared a suite, and Julia got her own room."

"I hope you all had a wonderful time." Celeste smiled.

"It was a fairy-tale wedding and so beautiful," Julia said.

"Thank you, Julia. I'm so happy you could join us."

The doors opened to the lobby, and we all stepped out.

"Have fun on your honeymoon, you two," I said.

"We will, son. The four of you stay out of trouble while we're gone."

"Always do, Dad," Sebastian said.

"Thanks for that." I placed my hand on Stefan's shoulder.

"You're welcome. I'll catch you guys later."

~

*J*ulia

After Sam dropped me off at home, I started cleaning and saved the living room for last. As I was dusting the console, I picked up the picture of Justin and stared at it. For the first time since he died, I felt at peace. What was happening between Sam and I was real. I felt it, and I know he did too. Grabbing my phone, I dialed my therapist and planned to leave a message until she picked up on the second ring.

"Julia Benton. It's been a long time."

"Hi, Doctor Strong. I didn't expect you to answer the phone."

"I'm here just catching up on some paperwork because

I'm leaving for vacation in a couple of days. Is something wrong?"

"No, not really. Well, maybe. I was just going to leave a message for your secretary to call me back so I could set up an appointment with you."

"Like I said, I'm going on vacation, and I'll be gone about a month. Dr. Cassidy is taking my patients while I'm gone. You know what? I'm here, and I plan on being here a while. Why don't you come by, and we'll have a session?"

"Are you sure?"

"Of course. When can you be here?"

"In about thirty minutes?"

"Sounds good. I'll see you then."

"Thank you, Dr. Strong."

"Don't mention it, Julia. I'll see you soon."

I hadn't seen Dr. Strong in about a year because I felt like I didn't need to keep seeing her. It had become more of a habit and the security of knowing I could talk to her without being judged. After a certain amount of time passes, people don't hesitate to throw their two cents in.

*"It's been long enough. You need to jump back into the dating game."*

*"You can find someone else. You're a beautiful girl. Stop hiding."*

*"Stop feeling sorry for yourself."*

*"It's time to let go. There's plenty of fish in the sea."*

*"You'll find love again. Just put yourself out there."*

I parked my car in front of her office building and went inside. When she heard the bell above the door ring, her office door opened.

"Julia, it's great to see you. Come in and sit down."

"Thanks, Dr. Strong."

"Coffee?" she asked.

"I'd love some."

She brewed a cup of coffee and handed it to me. Walking

over to her desk, she grabbed her notepad and sat down in the leather chair across from me.

"So, what's going on?"

"I've met someone, and he's becoming very special to me."

"Excellent. Tell me about him."

"He's actually my boss."

"Oh." Her face twisted. "Okay. Go on."

I told her about Steven Hart first. And then I told her about Sam, how we met, and the type of relationship we had.

"You've already taken the first step and admitted that you have feelings for him. For the first time in four years, you opened yourself up to someone and let your guard down. You're facing your fear of loss, Julia, and that's a big accomplishment. You're slowly climbing out of that hole of avoidance. I'm proud of you, and you should be too."

~

*I* brought the beer bottle up to my lips as the five of us sat around the bonfire and talked.

"Did Sammy tell you he has some wicked chops?"

"You sing?" I cocked my head at him with a smile.

"Thanks a lot, douchebag." He flung a bottle cap at him.

"How come I don't know this about you?"

"I guess it never came up." He shrugged.

"They sing too. Just not as good as me." He smirked.

"Truth, bro," Simon said.

"I want to hear you sing something," I begged.

"I'll go grab my guitar," Sebastian said.

"Bro, don't. Sit down," Sam spoke.

"The lady wants you to sing for her."

A few moments later, Sebastian returned and handed his guitar to Sam.

"Do I really have to do this?"

"Yes." I grinned as I sat back, brought my legs up, and listened to him as he played the guitar and sang the song "Collide."

The smile never left my face while he sang. When he finished the song, I clapped.

"Wow. You are amazing. I can't believe you never mentioned you can sing."

"Thanks."

He handed Sebastian his guitar back.

"Do all of you play the guitar?"

"Yeah, we do," Simon said. "We taught ourselves."

"Stefan, go get your ukulele and entertain us," Sam said.

"Be right back."

A few moments later, Stefan returned with his ukulele and sat down.

"Sing Lily's song for Julia," Sam said.

Stefan strummed his ukulele and sang, *Over the Rainbow*, Hawaiian style.

The smile never left my face as I glanced over at Sam, and he gave me a wink. My heart skipped a beat, and all I could think about was being wrapped up in his strong arms. After Stefan finished the song, Sebastian strummed a few chords of his guitar.

"Don't, Sebastian," Sam said with a warning.

"Aw, come on, bro. You know I love you." Sebastian looked at me with a wide grin on his handsome face. "This is Sam's song, and he hates when we sing it. This is how we feel, bro." Sebastian pointed at him.

"I fucking hate you." Sam let out a laugh.

He strummed the chords and sang "All the Pretty Girls" by Kaleo. Simon and Stefan joined in singing halfway through the song, and the three of them stood up and started jamming. When they finished, I jumped up from my chair and clapped with excitement. I was in awe of these four brothers.

"You guys are awesome. You should start your own band!"

"We thought about it once, and we practiced in the garage of our house. But we had other dreams to pursue," Stefan said.

"We just do it for fun," Simon spoke.

"It's been fun, my brothers, but it's time to call it a night," Sam said as he stood up from his chair. "Are you ready?" he asked.

"Yeah. I'm ready. Thanks for inviting me. I had the best time." I smiled as I looked at Simon, Stefan, and Sebastian.

"We loved having you here," Sebastian said.

"Maybe next time your sister can join us." The corners of Stefan's mouth curved upward.

"She'd love it. Good night, guys."

"Night, Julia. Night, Sam," all three of them spoke at the same time.

# CHAPTER 24

*Julia*

I opened my eyes and smiled as Sam's arm was securely wrapped around me. Carefully lifting his arm, I scooted out from under him, grabbed my bag, and quietly shut the bathroom door. When I finished throwing my clothes on, I opened the door and jumped when I saw Sam standing there.

"Were you just going to sneak out on me?" A smirk crossed his lips.

"No. I was going to leave a note."

"A note? Seriously?" He wrapped his arm around my waist and pulled me into him.

"We were practically up all night, and I didn't want to wake you."

"Well, my brothers just texted me to meet them down at the beach to go surfing."

"Have fun." I smiled as I kissed his lips. "If you don't mind, I'm going to make a cup of coffee before I leave. I'm not sure I'll be able to drive home without some caffeine first."

"Go ahead. And make me a cup while I get ready."

I set my bag down on the kitchen table and made us each a coffee. There was nothing more satisfying or soothing than that first sip.

"Your cup is right there." I pointed when Sam walked into the kitchen.

"Thanks." He opened the refrigerator and pulled out the cream. "You might want to turn around while I pour this in my coffee." He smirked.

"Shut up." I laughed. "I'd love for you to meet my sister. I mean, I know you met her over Facetime, but I'd like you to meet her in person."

"Just tell me when."

"Maybe tomorrow night you can come over for dinner? You don't have any appointments."

"I can do that." He took a few sips of his coffee. "I have to get down there. Have fun with your sister."

"Thanks. Have fun with your brothers."

"I will." He smiled as he walked out the sliding door.

I stood there and frowned for a moment because I thought he'd at least kiss me goodbye. Taking my cup over to the sliding door, I watched as the four of them gathered down at the beach and put their surfboards in the water. They were closer than any siblings could be, and their bond was very strong.

I headed home and unpacked my bag. Looking at the clock, Jenni's plane was scheduled to land in fifteen minutes. I wanted to pick her up from the airport, but she said the company she worked for had a car service waiting for her when she landed. Two hours later, the door to the apartment opened, and I heard Jenni's voice.

"I'm home, bitch!"

Running from my bedroom, I threw my arms around her.

"Welcome home!" I hugged her tight.

"God, Julia, it's so good to see you."

"I'm happy you're back. Go sit down. I made some chocolate chip cookies, and an unopened bottle of wine is waiting to be devoured over sisterly talk."

"Sounds delightful." She kicked off her shoes and sat down on the couch. "It's so good to be home."

"How was your trip?" I asked as I set a plate of cookies on the coffee table and handed my sister a glass of wine.

"It was a lot of work, but the sights were worth it. Enough about me. How are things going with Sam?"

"Things are good." I smiled.

She sat there and stared at me for a moment without saying a word.

"What?" I laughed.

"You're different. Oh my God, you've fallen for him, haven't you?"

"Maybe." I gave a bashful smile.

She set down her wine and gripped my arms.

"Julia Benton is in love!" She pulled me into her. "I'm so proud of you for letting someone into your life again."

"There's just one problem."

"What?" She broke our embrace.

"He doesn't get involved in relationships because of his parents. I went and saw Dr. Strong yesterday, and she told me he has avoidance anxiety and that I need to be patient and give him his space when he needs it. She also said not to take it personally when he needs to distance himself from me."

"Wait a minute. Are the two of you in more of a relationship than what you're telling me?"

"No. Not yet."

"Have you told him that you love him?"

"No. I'm kind of scared to tell him, considering he's never been in a relationship before."

"Then maybe it's best you keep that to yourself for a

while. Just wait and see how things go and how they progress."

"Yeah. I was thinking that too."

"I want to meet him in person."

"You are. He's coming over for dinner tomorrow night."

"Awesome. What are you going to make?"

"I thought maybe you could make your amazing bacon-wrapped pork tenderloin with those garlic whipped mashed potatoes since I have to work. Anything I make will have to be a quick dish."

"All right. I'll cook."

"Yay! Thank you. I love you." I hugged her.

"I love you too."

"Make sure you clean up as you cook. He's a total OCD clean freak."

"Really?" Her brows furrowed.

"Yeah. You should see his closets." I shook my head.

~

The next morning before I left for work, I received a text message from Sam.

*"Good morning. I have a few stops to make before heading to the office. I just wanted to let you know I'll be in later."*

*"Okay. I'll see you when you get there. Is there anything specific you want me to do?"*

*"Besides get naked and lay across my desk?"*

*"You're cute."* I sent him the rolling eyes emoji.

*"I know I am. I have a few things I want you to do while I'm gone. I'll text you a list."*

*"Okay. I still need to type up the Gatsby contract. It'll be finished by the time you get in."*

*"Sounds good. I'll see you later."*

As I was working on the contract, my phone rang, and Luciano Levers, Steven's attorney, was calling.

"Hello," I answered.

"Julia, it's Luciano Levers. How are you, my dear?"

"I'm good, Mr. Levers. How are you?"

"I'm good. Listen, can you come to my office this afternoon around four o'clock? Mr. Hart put you in his will, and since everything is now out of probate, it's time to give you what Steven wanted you to have."

"Wow. Really? Um, yes. I can be at your office at four o'clock."

"Excellent. I'll see you then, Julia."

I ended the call and sat there for a moment while I processed what Mr. Levers said. I was in shock that Steven put me in his will. I finished the contract and went to the ladies' room. When I got back, I saw Sam sitting behind his desk.

"Hey," I said as I walked in.

"There you are." The corners of his mouth curved upward.

"I was in the bathroom."

"Not vomiting, I hope." He smirked.

"No." I laughed. "The Gatsby contract is done. All I have to do is print it."

"Good. Before you do that, why don't you shut the door."

"Okay." I walked over to the door, and as I began to shut it, I felt Sam's hand on my hip while the other hand met mine as I closed the door. He lowered his hand, locked it, and then closed the blinds.

# CHAPTER 25

*J*ulia

"Did you think I was kidding when I said I wanted you naked and laying across my desk?" he whispered in my ear, making my body tremble.

"Somehow, I knew you weren't joking."

His tongue slid across my neck as his hand groped my breast. His other hand slid up the back of my skirt, and his fingers pushed my panties to the side. I gasped as he entered me and tilted my head to the side, giving him more access to my neck.

"You're already so wet. Do you know how much that turns me on?"

"Tell me," I moaned.

"It makes my cock as hard as a rock, and it throbs until it's buried deep inside your warm, wet pussy.

My moans grew louder as his fingers pulsated inside me. I would never get used to the intoxicating feeling that over-took me every time I was with him.

"As soon as you come, I'm going to turn you around, take

off your blouse and give your beautiful breasts the attention they deserve."

An orgasm took over me as he spoke those words. My body trembled with delight as his hand that groped my breast moved over my mouth to keep me from screaming.

"There you go. Good girl. Your orgasms turn me on so bad."

He turned me around and smashed his mouth against mine as his fingers unbuttoned my blouse. Slipping it off my shoulders, he tossed it to the ground along with my bra. His mouth left mine and traveled down to my breast while my fingers tangled in his hair.

"I need you right now, Julia."

"I need you too, Sam."

He led me over to his desk and told me to bend over. After taking down his pants, he pushed my skirt up and took down my panties. I let out a gasp as he pushed his way inside me. The heat inside me rose quickly as he swiftly moved in and out of me. Our moans were in sync with each other's as we both reached the state of orgasm together. Lowering my head, I tried to get my natural breathing rhythm back. He placed his hands on the desk next to mine and dropped his chin on my shoulder while trying to calm his breath. He pulled out of me and pulled up his pants while I pulled up my panties and lowered my skirt.

"Here." He smiled as he handed me my bra and blouse.

"Thank you."

While I finished dressing, he took a seat behind his desk.

"I need to see those contracts now."

"I'll go print them out," I said as I walked to the door. "By the way, I need to leave early today. I have a four o'clock appointment."

"Okay. Sure. That shouldn't be a problem."

When I opened the door, Stefan was walking by. He

stopped and turned around as I ran my hands through my hair.

"Did you and Sam just—" He moved his finger from side to side.

"I don't know what you're talking about," I nervously spoke and went over to my desk.

"Judging that your blouse is buttoned wrong, I would say you did." He smirked, and I looked down.

"Shit."

Stefan let out a laugh.

"Don't worry about it. I won't tell." He gave me a wink and walked down the hallway.

$\sim$

"*I* need to head out now," I said to Sam as I stepped into his office.

"Okay. I'll see you later at your place." He smiled.

"By the way, my sister is cooking a fabulous dinner since I'm working all day."

"I'm sure it'll be delicious."

I climbed in my car and headed to Mr. Levers office. When I arrived, he took me into the conference room, where I saw Gina sitting at the table.

"Gina?" I grinned.

"Julia." She stood up and hugged me. "It's been a while."

"I know, and I'm so sorry. I've been really busy with work."

"I understand."

"Please, Julia, have a seat," Mr. Levers spoke. "As I mentioned over the phone, Steven left you something in his will. He wanted me to read this to you when the time came.

*Julia,*

*You were a godsend that day in the restaurant. If you weren't there, I'm not sure I would have survived. I always told you that you were an angel sent from God. Not only did you save my life, but you were also the best personal assistant anyone could ever ask for. In the three and a half years you worked for me, Gina and I considered you a part of our family. But you already knew that because we told you numerous times. I could never repay you enough for saving my life that day, and I hope by me giving you your dream, that will be payment enough. I, Steven Grant Hart, give Julia Marie Benton full ownership of the building located at 311 Sunset Blvd. in Venice, California. It's time for you to make your dream come true, Julia. Open your coffee café and live life to the fullest. Never stop dreaming, my friend.*

    *Love,*

    *Steven*

I placed my hand over my mouth and looked at Gina, who sat there with tears in her eyes and a smile on her face. Instantly, the tears that swelled in my eyes began to fall.

"I don't know what to say. I'm in shock right now."

"You don't have to say anything, Julia. All you have to do is do what Steven wanted."

"Julia," Mr. Levers spoke, "Steven also left you a lump sum of money in his trust to get the shop up and running. All you need to do is submit all expenses to me, and they will be paid. You'll need someone to design the inside, and then you'll have to hire a crew to come in and build it. I can give you some names."

"Thank you. I already know a great company that can do it."

"Great. I'll get all the paperwork submitted, and I'll bring you the keys in a few days."

"Thank you, Mr. Levers."

"You're welcome, Julia. If you'll both excuse me, I have other business to attend to."

Gina reached across the table and took hold of my hand.

"He wanted this for you."

"Why did he recommend me to Sam Kind if he was giving me the building?" I asked.

"Because he knew it would take a while to get everything sorted out, and he didn't want you to be jobless. You can still work for Mr. Kind while your café is under construction. Do you know what you're going to call it yet?"

"I've always liked Mojo Madness. You know how everyone needs their coffee, and if they don't get it, it kind of creates a madness until they do."

"I love it, and I can't wait to see it. You call me if you need anything. Do you understand me?"

"Thank you, Gina. I appreciate it, and I will."

We both stood up from our seats and walked out of the conference room.

"Let's meet for lunch or dinner next week. It's up to you," Gina said.

"Definitely. I'll call you." I gave her a hug.

As I walked to my car, I was on cloud nine. I couldn't believe Steven had done that for me. I was finally going to own and run my own coffee shop. I was so excited, and I couldn't wait to get home and tell Jenni. Then reality set in, and I came down from my high. I wouldn't be working for Sam anymore, and I wasn't sure how he would take it. He'd be excited for me, right? He knew this had always been a dream of mine, and as close as we were, he would be happy for me. But I needed to wait to tell him. I needed time to process everything and make a plan.

# CHAPTER 26

## THREE DAYS LATER

*S*am

Julia spent the night at my house since her sister had a visitor last night. I liked Jenni. She reminded me of Julia. As I was sitting at my desk, I took note of the paperweight that seemed out of place. I'd already adjusted it twice this week, and then it hit me.

"Julia!"

"Yes." She walked in with a sexy smile.

"Have you been messing with my paperweight?"

She began to laugh, and I knew right then she did.

"I just had to see if you'd notice. Sam, I barely moved it." She continued to laugh. "A normal person never would have noticed."

I sat there and cocked my head at her.

"You're coming to my place tonight, and I'll take the rest of the day to think about how I'm going to reprimand you."

"Reprimand me? For touching your paperweight?" Her brow arched. "Bring it on, boss man."

"Oh, I will. Don't worry."

"I'm not worried. I'm intrigued."

My cock was starting to rise because her mere words turned me on.

"You need to get back to work." I shifted in my chair.

"In all seriousness, I was going to ask you if I could come over tonight. There's something I want to talk to you about."

"Okay. You can talk to me after your punishment."

"I look forward to it." She flashed a sexy smile as she walked out of my office.

I let out a deep breath and leaned back in my chair. My phone rang, and when I picked it up, I saw Ken was calling.

"Hey, Ken."

"Sam. You will never believe what I'm about to tell you."

"What?"

"I found out whom Steven Hart left the building on Sunset Blvd to, and it's not his wife."

"Who is it?"

"Julia Benton, your personal assistant."

"What?" I quickly sat up. "Are you sure?"

"Positive. I heard it from my own attorney's mouth. I want that building, Sam, and you're going to get it for me. You do whatever you have to. Sweet talk her, marry her, whatever. Because if you don't, our contract is done, and I will give the outdoor mall and hospital to someone else. I won't be the only one losing out here. Your company will lose millions of dollars from me alone. You know I always get what I want, Sam."

"Don't worry, Ken. I'll get you the building."

"I know you will. I'll be in touch."

*Click.*

I slowly set my phone down and rubbed my face with my hands. I couldn't believe Julia didn't tell me. Maybe that's what she wanted to talk about tonight. Why the hell would Steven leave her an empty building?

"Oh shit," I said out loud.

He gave her that building so she could open a coffee shop. Fuck!

~

"Hey, bro," Stefan said as he walked inside my kitchen through the sliding door.

"Right now isn't a good time. Julia is on her way over."

"Okay? And?"

"I said it's not a good time," I shouted with irritation.

"Hey, calm the fuck down. What's going on with you?"

"Ken called me today. You know that building he wants?"

"Yeah. The one over on Sunset Blvd.? What about it?"

"It turns out Steven Hart left it to Julia in his will."

"Our Julia?" He asked, and I shot him a look. "Does Julia know?"

"Yes, she knows, and she hasn't told me yet. But she said she had something to talk to me about tonight, and I suspect it's about the building."

"Okay. What's the big deal?"

"Ken told me that if I don't get Julia to sell it to him, he's pulling out and taking the outdoor mall and hospital with him. We're talking millions and millions of dollars, Stefan."

"He wouldn't do that. He's been with us for over ten years. Who else is going to kiss his ass the way we do?"

"You should have heard the tone in his voice."

"Why does he want that building so badly?"

"Because his wife wants it for her shop. She's been harping on him for a year about it."

"Oh. Delilah is a bitch, too. Poor guy."

"No. Poor me!" I jammed my finger into my chest.

"I think you're getting yourself all worked up over nothing. What the hell is Julia going to do with an empty building? Ken can make her a very rich woman."

"Her dream has always been to open a coffee shop of her own. And now, Steven made that possible for her. She's not going to give up that building."

"She might. You don't know that until you talk to her. But you better stay calm about it." He pointed at me. "The worst thing you can do is piss her off."

I heard a car pull into the driveway.

"She's here. You better go."

"Okay. Keep me posted, and remember, stay calm."

I took a deep breath as I walked over and opened the door.

"Hey." I smiled as I brushed my lips against hers.

"Hi."

"Can I pour you a drink?"

"A glass of wine will do." The corners of her mouth curved upward. "Have you thought about how you're going to reprimand me for touching your paperweight?"

"I have, and we can discuss that later. What did you want to talk about? You sounded kind of serious?" I handed her a glass of wine and poured myself a scotch.

"We can talk about that later." She ran her finger down my chest.

"No. I would like to talk about it now."

She narrowed her eye at me for a moment and took in a deep breath.

"Remember when I left early the other day for an appointment?"

"Yes. I remember."

"It was with Luciano Levers, Steven's attorney. Steven put me in his will." She smiled.

"That was nice of him. What did he leave you?"

"A building over on Sunset Blvd. Actually, it's about five minutes from here."

I couldn't keep the fact that I already knew about it a secret anymore.

"I know, Julia."

"You do? How?"

"Ken called me this afternoon and told me."

"Ken, who?"

"Ken Kramer, our client."

"Oh. Well, it's finally happening, Sam. I'm going to open my very own coffee shop. But I don't want you to worry. I'll still work for you until it's ready, and I'll help you find another assistant, and I'll train them."

"Whoa, slow down. So, you are going to go ahead with the coffee shop plan?"

"Of course, I am. You know it's been my dream."

"Julia, you don't know anything about running a business."

"Sam." Her voice was serious. "I know things. I practically ran the coffee shop I worked at."

"There's a big difference between being an assistant manager and an owner."

"Are you saying that I can't do it and that I'll fail?"

I let out a sigh as I rubbed the back of my head.

# CHAPTER 27

*J*ulia

"Well?" I stood there in disbelief.

"Yeah, Julia, that is what I'm saying. There are thousands of coffee shops in this city, and everyone and their brother is opening one up. It's hard to get a trendy business like that off the ground. I just don't want to see you get in over your head."

"Wow. Thanks for the confidence, boss."

"Listen." He walked over and ran the back of his hand down my cheek. "Ken Kramer wants that building. He's been trying to get it since Steven bought it. He will make you a very rich woman if you sell it to him. You won't even have to work."

I took a step back because I couldn't believe he said those things to me.

"This isn't about money. This is about me finally being able to live my dream." A frown overtook my face. "This is about what I want and have always wanted, Sam. You and your brothers are living your dreams, Jenni is doing what she's always wanted to do, and I'm just stuck in limbo."

"You can't look at it that way."

"But I do. This is my chance to open a business I always wanted to open, and you're dismissing it as if it's nothing. Do you even realize how important this is to me?"

"I do. But I don't think it's a good idea. I think you need to sell the building to Ken."

"Well, I'm not!" I shouted. "I'm opening my fucking coffee shop. Ken Kramer can find another building to buy! And who are you to tell me what I can and can't do? You're not my boyfriend or my husband."

"Julia, calm down. Please." He rubbed his forehead.

"No. I won't calm down! I thought you'd be happy for me. I know I'd be happy for you if the situation was reversed."

"It was a nice thought and gesture. But you need to step into reality, Julia."

"I am, Sam. Do you think I'm just a dumb personal assistant who can't do anything else?"

"No. Of course not. I know you're smart. You're very smart."

"Then what is this really about? Is it the fact that I won't be working for you anymore?"

"No. You're replaceable."

"Excuse me?" I could feel the tears sting my eyes.

"That came out wrong."

"No. I don't think it did, Samuel."

"Don't you ever call me that again." He shook his finger at me.

"And don't you tell me to sell my building."

"God, Julia!" He threw his arms out. "You have no idea how this will hurt me!" he shouted.

I walked over to him and placed my hand on his chest.

"Nothing has to change between us. We can still see each other every day."

His brows furrowed at me. "What the hell are you talking about?"

"Us."

"WHAT! There is no 'us,' Julia!"

"But you just said that this is going to hurt you."

He lowered his head and pinched the top of his nose as he paced around the room.

"Listen to me very carefully. If you don't sell that building to Ken, he's pulling out, and we're going to lose millions and millions of dollars. Can you comprehend that for fuck's sake?"

"What? Did he tell you that?"

"YES!"

"So that's what this is about. You and the company. You don't give a damn about me, what I want, or how I feel."

"I care about my company, Julia. Not your damn dream about opening a stupid coffee shop."

Suddenly, the air grew thick, and I found it difficult to breathe.

"You bastard. How dare you?"

"Please, Julia. Just sell him the damn building, and we can put all this behind us. You can open a coffee shop up somewhere else. I'll even help you find a building."

"No. Steven left that building to me. He wanted me to put my coffee shop there, in that building!"

"Damn it, Julia!" he shouted.

"You're choosing money over me."

"Of course, I am! Why would you think I wouldn't?"

"Maybe because I thought you cared about me."

I braced myself for the next words that came out of his mouth.

"Care about you?" He chuckled. "Yeah. I care a little, but not enough to justify losing millions of dollars because you're being stubborn."

"What about all the time we spend together outside of the office?" A tear fell down my cheek.

"I need you to sell that building, Julia." His tone was authoritative.

"And I need you to stand there and tell me that you don't feel something for me."

Our eyes stared at each other as a moment of silence filled the air.

"If I told you I did, would you sell it?"

"No. I wouldn't."

"Well, I guess I don't have to lie to you then."

"You're unbelievable." I shook my head as the tears fell from my eyes.

"If you think those tears are going to make me feel bad, they don't. You are nothing to me but my personal assistant and a girl I fuck. That's it. That's all you ever were. Nothing but a good time."

"You bastard." I raised my hand to him, and he grabbed my wrist.

"I hate you, Sam Kind. I've never hated anyone in my life, but I can stand here and say that I truly hate you and the man you are. I can't believe I fell in love with you!"

I grabbed my purse and headed for the door.

"Don't you dare open that door!" he shouted. "We aren't finished."

"The hell we're not." I scurried out the door.

"Julia, get back here!" He ran after me, and Simon ran up and held him back.

"By the way, I quit! Find yourself another assistant you can fuck and feel nothing for!"

My car was locked, and I stood there shaking uncontrollably, trying to find my key in my purse.

"Julia," Sebastian ran up to me. "Let me drive you home."

"No. I'm fine." I wiped my eyes.

"No. You're not. You're shaking."

"I'm okay, Sebastian. Please, just leave me alone."

After finally finding my key, I unlocked the car, climbed inside, and peeled out of his driveway.

# CHAPTER 28

*S*am
"What the fuck, Sam!" Sebastian shouted.

"You're lucky Lily isn't home and witnessed that. I would have beat your ass!" Stefan said. "What the hell happened to staying calm?"

I jerked myself out of Simon's grip, went back inside the house, and poured myself a double scotch.

"Bro, what the hell?" Simon said.

"I take it she's not selling the building to Ken?" Stefan said. "And now you're out another assistant."

"I don't need to hear this right now." I threw back my drink.

"She was shaking like crazy, Sam. What the hell did you say to her?" Sebastian asked.

"It doesn't matter."

"It does matter!" Sebastian shouted. "You just ruined the best thing that has ever happened to you! And for what? Money? Damn it, Sam." He shook his head.

"Listen, I appreciate the brotherly love, but I really want to be alone right now."

"Too fucking bad," Stefan said. "You weren't alone in the womb, and you're not alone right now. You're our brother, and we're hurting too."

"Yeah, bro." Simon hooked his arm around me. "You know when one of us is hurting, we all hurt."

"She said something to me that I can't shake."

"What did she say?" Stefan asked.

"She said she can't believe she fell in love with me."

"Damn," Sebastian said. "What did you say to her?"

"A lot of bad and hurtful things." I took my drink over to the couch and sat down.

~

*J*ulia

The second I pulled out of his driveway, my phone rang, and Jenni was calling.

"Jenni," I cried.

"Julia, I knew it. What's wrong?"

"Are you home?"

"Yes. I'm here."

"I'm on my way. I'll tell you everything when I get home."

"Okay. Drive safe."

I couldn't stop shaking for the life of me. His words kept replaying over and over in my head. The tears fell freely, and I couldn't stop them. The pain. The agonizing pain of a broken heart. I was so stupid for letting him in. Stupid for thinking he had feelings for me or cared about me.

I'd finally made it home, and the second I opened the apartment door, Jenni was right there to hold me up. She held me tight, and I sobbed on her shoulder.

"There, there. Let it all out. And when you calm down, you're going to tell me what happened."

She walked me to the bedroom, where I curled up on my bed.

"I hate him so much, Jenni."

"Who? Sam?"

I nodded my head as she handed me a tissue.

"What the hell happened?"

Through all the tears, I managed to tell her everything he said.

"I'm going to that office tomorrow and pick up the things you left there," she said.

"Please don't say anything if you see him," I begged.

"I won't because I might end up killing him if I do. You listen to me, Julia Marie. I'm allowing you twenty-four hours to grieve over this. After that, you'll pick yourself up and start making plans for Mojo Madness."

"I was going to ask him to help me with the design and hire Stefan to do the inside. Now, what do I do?"

"That asshole isn't the only architect in L.A., Julia. We'll find someone and a good contractor."

"Will you sleep with me tonight?" I asked her.

"You know I already am." A sympathetic smile crossed her lips. Get in your jammies, and I'll go get in mine. Then I'll grab the carton of Rocky Road from the freezer, a couple of spoons, and we'll watch some cheesy Lifetime or Hallmark movie, and this situation you're dealing with won't seem so bad after all."

I couldn't help but let out a light laugh.

~

*S*am
After my brothers went home, I got my guitar out from the closet and strummed some chords. Something inside me felt off, and I set my guitar down. I couldn't stop

thinking about the tears that streamed down her face, the sadness and hurt in her eyes, and the pain in her voice as she shouted at me. I felt like an asshole. She was right. I was a bastard, and I shouldn't have said the things I did. But the reality was that when it came down to it, my business always had to come first. I poured myself another drink, took it upstairs to the balcony off my bedroom, sat down, and stared out into the ocean as a tear ran down my cheek.

The next morning, I woke up earlier than usual, grabbed my surfboard, and put it in the water.

"Want some company?"

I turned around and saw Simon standing there.

"Sure."

He put his board in and paddled out to me.

"How did you sleep last night?" he asked.

"Like shit."

"You know, Sam—"

"I don't want to hear it, Simon. It is what it is now. She should never have fallen in love with me."

"And you shouldn't have led her on the way you did. Or maybe you weren't leading her on. Nobody keeps sleeping with the same person over and over and has no feelings for them."

"Doesn't matter anymore." I looked away. "I should head back and get ready for work."

"Have a good day, bro." He patted my back.

"It won't be." I paddled back to the shore.

When I arrived at the office, I stopped at Julia's desk and picked up the small frame that held a picture of her and her sister. A sick feeling washed over me, so I set it down and went to grab a cup of coffee from the break room.

"Good morning, Sam." Grayson smiled as he patted my back before he opened the refrigerator.

"Morning."

"Hey. Is Julia in yet? I need to ask her something."

"No."

"When is she coming in?" He glanced over at me as he stirred his yogurt.

"She's not." I opened the refrigerator and grabbed the cream.

"You mean she's not coming in today, right?"

"No, Grayson. Julia quit."

"Jesus Christ, Sam! When did she do that?"

"Yesterday."

"Can you give me a little more information than just a couple of words?"

"She's opening a coffee shop."

"Phew. Good for her. I thought you were going to tell me it had to do with you."

"It did."

"Damn it, Sam! Talk to me."

"We got into a huge fight because I told her she needed to sell the building that Steven Hart left her to Ken Kramer. She said no, I became angry and said some things I shouldn't have."

"You've been sleeping with her, haven't you?"

"Yes. I never stopped after the first time. She was good with it. She loved it. Then she thought—it doesn't matter. She's gone, and I'm putting the brakes on a personal assistant for a while. I'll use one of the other girls until I figure something out."

"Good. I'm happy to hear you say that. I'm sorry about Julia. I really liked her." He walked out of the break room.

I was sitting in my office when Joan walked in.

"Where's Julia, Sam?"

"She quit, Joan."

"Just like that? No two weeks or anything?"

"No. She quit yesterday."

"Dumb, dumb man you are, Samuel Kind." She shook her head. "Out of all the assistants that come and go around here, you had to let that one go?"

"It's complicated."

"It's always complicated with you, Sam." She walked out of my office.

I'd never felt so low as I did today. While I was sitting at my drafting table, my phone rang. It was the call I'd been waiting for all day.

"Ken, how are you?"

"I'd be better if I'd heard from you by now, Sam."

"Sorry about that. It's been a crazy day."

"Well? Did you tell Julia to sell me the building?"

"I did, and she said no. She's opening a coffee shop."

"So that's it? Why am I under the impression you didn't make it clear to her what would happen if I didn't get it."

"I told her, we got in a huge argument, and she quit. She is no longer an employee here. There's nothing more I can do, Ken. I'm sorry. I tried."

"Obviously, not hard enough. The one thing I'm not sorry for is leaving Kind Design & Architecture behind. My outdoor mall and hospital will be going to another firm."

"I think you're making a mistake, but you do what you feel you have to."

"I am. Kramer Enterprises and Kind Architecture will no longer be doing business effective immediately. Goodbye, Sam."

He ended the call before I had the chance to say anything else. Just as I threw my phone across the room, Stefan walked into my office.

"Whoa. You're going to break it," he said as he walked over and picked my phone up.

"I don't care. That was Ken. He's done with us effective immediately."

"He's a shady motherfucker, Sam. If he's going to do that over a stupid building for his wife, he's not worth it."

"Do you understand the money we just lost?" I narrowed my eye at him.

"Yes. I do understand. But we have a lot of other clients, and we take new ones on all the time."

"Ken was a major client. Losing him could send this company on a spiraling downfall."

"That's not going to happen. You're overthinking things. Let it go and move on."

"Dad's going to be pissed when he finds out. He's handing over the company to us in a few months, and this is how we thank him?"

"It's not your fault. And if you want my honest opinion, you never should have asked Julia to sell."

"I don't want your opinion." I scowled at him.

"You chose the business over her. Maybe that was always dad's problem and why he's been married so many times. But if you noticed, Celeste is different in his eyes. He took more time off since he'd met her than ever before. And now he's retiring."

"Of course, I chose the business over her. She was nothing to me but an employee."

"Keep telling yourself that to make yourself feel better. I have to go. I'll be home tonight if you want to come over."

I heard Stefan talking to someone outside my office, so I got up to see who was there. Opening my door, I was shocked to see Jenni standing there with a small box. The moment she saw me, rage filled her eyes.

"You can go back inside your office. I'm only here to collect Julia's personal things."

"Jenni—"

"Don't you say a fucking word to me, Sam."

I slowly went back inside my office and shut the door. A few moments later, the door flew open, and Jenni walked in.

"How could you do that to my sister?" she shouted. "Do you know what she's going through right now because of you?"

"I'm sorry, but—"

"I don't want to hear your damn excuses. She told me everything and every word that came out of your mouth! You used her all this time for your own satisfaction."

"Your sister was a willing participant!" I shouted.

"She fell in love with you, and you made her feel like a whore! You don't care about her or what she wants. The only thing you care about is money. And that's the difference between the two of you. Julia has a soul, and you don't." She stormed out of my office.

# CHAPTER 29

*J*ulia

When I started the shower, I stood there naked and stared at it. Grabbing a towel, I wrapped it around me, sunk to the floor, and leaned my body against the tub as I brought my knees up to my chest. I'd felt as if I was drowning, and I couldn't make my way back to the surface. They say loss is loss, no matter how it happened. I lost Sam, but was he ever really mine to begin with? Little by little, he crept his way into my heart, and I let him. Like a damn fool, I let him. Jenni told me that everything happens for a reason, and Sam was just the first step to show me that I could love someone again. To me it showed stupidity and a big slap in the face telling me, "I told you so. Why would you even think about loving anyone again?"

After a few tears fell, I picked myself up and climbed into the shower. After getting dressed, I walked to the kitchen and heard the door open.

"Here are your things." She smiled as she set the box down on the table.

"Did you see him?"

"For a brief moment."

"And?"

"Nothing. I grabbed your things and left."

"He didn't say anything to you. You didn't say anything to him?"

"Nope." She shook her head.

"Mom's been calling, and I haven't been answering."

"I know. She called me. I told her you've been super busy and have exciting news to tell her and dad. We're going over there for dinner tonight."

"Damn it, Jenni. I'm not leaving this apartment."

"Yes, you are, Julia. You need to tell Mom and Dad about the coffee shop. You don't have to tell them what happened with Sam."

"And if I start crying in front of them?"

"They'll be tears of joy over the building Steven left you. I got your back, sis. Don't worry." She hugged me.

≈

One Week Later

*A*s I unlocked the door to my building, I heard someone call my name.

"Julia?"

Turning around, I saw Stefan standing there in a pair of jogging pants and a t-shirt.

"Hey, Stefan."

"I thought that was you. This is it?" he pointed to the building.

"Yeah. This is it."

"Would you mind if I took a look inside?"

"Not at all. Come in."

"Wow. Great space. Have you hired a contractor yet?"

"I'm meeting with Witt Design & Construction in a few minutes. He just called, and he's on his way."

"Oh. Mind if I stick around?"

"No. Not at all."

"How are you, Julia?"

"I'm great." I put on a brave smile. "How are you doing?"

"I'm good. Sam is—"

"I don't want to hear his name." I put my hand up.

"That's understandable. I'm sorry. Listen, Julia, what went down with you and him has nothing to do with us, and we like you, and that hasn't changed."

"Thanks, Stefan. I appreciate it."

"Miss Benton?" A man walked into the building.

"Yes. Mr. Witt?"

"You can call me Bill." He extended his hand. "Stefan Kind. What are you doing here?"

"Hello, Bill. Julia is a friend of mine."

"I see. Then why aren't you doing the work?"

"It's complicated," he said. "Go ahead with your meeting, and don't mind me."

Bill and I walked the space, and I told him exactly what I was thinking about doing.

"Yeah. That's not going to work," Bill said.

"Sure, it will, Bill," Stefan intervened. "You just have to know what you're doing."

Bill ignored what Stefan had said, and we continued our meeting. He gave me his estimated price, and Stefan started laughing.

"What is so funny?" Bill asked.

"You're totally ripping her off, Bill. Just like with the Canton project. Why do you think we got the job instead?"

"You know what? I'm out of here. I'm sorry, Miss Benton, but my company won't be able to help you out. I'm sorry." He walked away.

"Bill, wait!"

"Let him go, Julia. That guy is a crook."

"Thanks a lot, Stefan. It took me a week to get him to come out here."

"I'll do it, and it'll cost half of what he would charge you."

"No." I shook my head. "I can't hire you."

"Yes, you can. You know the company and me, and you trust us."

"What about Sam? He won't do the designs, and he certainly won't be happy about you doing the work."

"I'll do the design, and you don't worry about him. I'll handle Sam."

I took in a deep breath as he went to his car to get a notepad. I knew this was the worst idea possible, but he was right. I did trust him and his company.

~

"*A*nd over here is where I want a small stage."

"A stage?" he asked in confusion.

"So people can come and play music here." I smiled.

"Okay. We'll put a stage here."

"And I want the entire front and side nothing but windows. I want it to be bright and inviting."

"Okay. Lots and lots of windows. Got it." He smiled as he looked up from his notepad. "This is a great space for a coffee shop, and it will be amazing. I can't wait to get started."

"Steven knew about my vision. We talked about it all the time. When we'd be driving to or from a meeting, we'd always stop and get a coffee. I would look around and tell him what I would do differently in my shop. He cared. Unlike some people." I looked down.

Stefan placed his hand on my shoulder and gave it a gentle squeeze.

# CHAPTER 30

*S*am

"Got a minute?" Stefan said as he popped his head into my office.

"Yeah. What's up?" I leaned back in my chair.

"I ran into Julia this morning."

"Where at?"

"Her building. I was going for a run, and I saw her unlocking the door."

"And you're telling me this why?"

"While I was there, Bill Witt dropped in to give her a quote."

"Witt? Are you kidding me?" I chuckled.

"He got all pissed off when I was putting in my two cents, and he walked out."

"The guy is a total douchebag," I said.

"I offered Julia my help with the shop."

"You what?!" I shouted.

"Calm down, bro."

"The hell I will! You have no right, Stefan."

"Why? What happened between the two of you was your

fault, and it has nothing to do with me, Sam."

"It does since you're part owner of this company. You're going to do work for the woman that cost us millions of dollars?"

"Jesus Christ. Give it up already. Julia didn't cost this company a dime. Ken Kramer did because he's an asshole, and you know it!" He pointed at me.

I immediately stood up from my seat and walked over to him.

"What is this really about, Stefan?"

"What the hell are you talking about?"

"You helping Julia out? You have a thing for her?"

"Don't be a dick, Sam. What the hell is wrong with you?" he shouted.

Taking my finger, I jammed it into his chest.

"You had a thing for her from the day you met her."

"You're fucking crazy, man. I have not. And you better get your finger off me."

"Just admit it."

"I don't have a thing for Julia, and if I did, so what? She's not yours. You made sure to fuck that up."

I balled my fist and punched him in the face. The next thing I knew, he swung back and hit me right in the jaw. We went at it until Simon ran in and broke us up.

"What the hell is going on in here?! Enough!" Simon broke us up. "What is the matter with you two?"

"He started it," Stefan said.

"The hell I did." I wiped the blood from my lip.

"Stefan, go. And get some ice for your face."

Stefan shook his head and walked out of my office.

"You better get some ice on yourself as well."

"What are you doing here, Simon?"

"I was in the area, and I thought I'd stop by and see my dumbass brothers. It's a good thing I did, or else the two of you might have killed each other. What is going on?"

"Stefan is helping Julia with her shop, and I know he's doing it because he wants to get in her pants."

"For God's sake, Sam. He does not. We're not teenagers anymore. We're grown men. I think that's what you want to believe so you can be pissed off at the world."

~

*I* was sitting out on the deck having a drink when I saw Stefan walking towards my house.

"Hey," he said. "Can I have one of those?" he pointed to my glass.

"Help yourself. You know where it is."

A few moments later, he walked back out and sat down in the chair next to me.

"I had to tell Lily we were play wrestling, and we got carried away."

"Good thinking. I'll make sure to tell her the same thing if she asks. I'm sorry I hit you."

"I'm sorry too. I shouldn't have said what I did."

"I miss her, Stefan."

"I know you do." He placed his hand on my shoulder.

"How was she? Does she seem okay?"

"I think she was putting on a front for me. But I could tell she wasn't her usual vibrant and happy self."

"I take it you're doing the design?"

"I am. She has some great ideas."

"Did you give her a deal?"

"Yeah. I did."

"Good."

"It doesn't have to be like this, Sam. Go apologize to her and work it out."

"I can't. She's better off without me in her life."

"That's not true."

"It is, brother. She's been hurt enough in her life already. She doesn't deserve it." It took everything I had inside me to hold back the tears that were coming.

"It's okay, Sam. Let it out. You don't have to go through this alone."

I swallowed hard as I inhaled a deep breath.

"Let me do the design, and you'll tell her you did it. At least I'll feel like I'm righting my wrongs in some way."

"Are you sure?"

"Yeah." I wiped my eyes. "I want to do it."

"Okay. I have the blueprint of the building at the house. I was going to work on it tonight. I'll go get it."

"Thanks, Stefan."

We both stood up from our seats and hugged each other.

"It'll be okay, bro. Just hang in there."

I went inside the house, poured myself another drink, and set it on my drafting table in my office. A few moments later, Stefan walked in and handed me the blueprint.

"Here are all the notes I took on what she wants."

"Thanks. I'll start working on it now. Did you give her a timeframe?"

"I told her I'd have it in a couple of days."

"I'll have it done by tomorrow, even if it takes me all night."

As I looked over his notes, I noticed she wanted a small stage. Picking up my phone, I called Stefan.

"What's up, bro?"

"Am I reading this right? She wants a stage built-in?"

"Yeah. She wants a space where people can come and play music. That's all she said. I don't know all the details."

"Okay. I'll put one in for her."

# CHAPTER 31

*J*ulia

"I hate leaving you again," Jenni said as she hugged me goodbye.

"I'll be fine. You won't be gone very long."

"Damn right, I won't be. And when I get back, we're going to hit the town up." She smiled.

"Have a safe flight, and I'll see you in a couple of weeks."

"I'll be calling you every day, and when I do, you better answer."

"I will." The corners of my mouth curved upward. "I love you."

"I love you, too, sis. I'll be back soon."

I'd always felt a sadness when Jenni left for one of her trips. But this time was harder than all the other times because I was already so sad over Sam. As I was pondering my thoughts, my phone rang, and Stefan was calling.

"Hi, Stefan."

"Hi, Julia. I have the design done. I can meet you at the shop whenever you're available."

"That's great. Depending on traffic, I can meet in about thirty minutes if that's okay."

"I'll see you there," he said.

I put my shoes on, grabbed my keys and purse, and headed out the door. When I arrived at the shop, Stefan was waiting for me.

"Oh my God, what happened to you?" I asked as I stared at his face.

"It's nothing. You should see the other guy." His lips gave way to a smirk.

I unlocked the door, and when we stepped inside, Stefan laid out the design on the folding table that sat in the middle of the space. We went over the plan, and it was perfect.

"Stefan, this is amazing. You did such a good job on this. You should design more often."

"Thanks, but I like to build."

"Does Sam know what you're doing?" I asked. But I already knew the answer.

"Yeah. I told him."

"Now the bruises on your face make more sense." I looked down. "Listen, let's just forget this. I will not be the reason you and your brother are fighting."

"Julia, stop. Trust me. It has nothing to do with this. I said something to him that I shouldn't have. Anyway, he apologized, and we're good. This isn't the first time we've fought. All of us have taken each other down over the years." He smiled. "It's what brothers do."

"Can you do me a favor?" I asked as I pulled my keys from my purse.

"Of course."

"Can you give Sam back his key? I forgot to give it to Jenni when she went to the office to collect my things."

"Yeah. I'll give it to him." He took the key from me and gave me a sympathetic smile. "Are you sure you don't want to go over there while he's at work and mess up things in the house?"

I let out a laugh. "Don't tempt me."

～

*S*am
I was sitting behind my desk scrolling through the pictures on my phone when I came across a few of Julia when we were in Montauk. I took them when I was taking photos of the land Casey purchased. Only she didn't know I took them.

"Sam?" Joan popped her head through the door. "Your father wants to see you and Stefan."

"He's in today?" I furrowed my brows.

"Yeah. I was surprised as well. He's in his office."

"Thanks, Joan. I'll let Stefan know."

As I was on my way to Stefan's office, I saw him step off the elevator.

"Are you just getting in?" I asked.

"Yeah. I just came from meeting Julia."

"And?"

"She loved the design, and then she tried to fire me."

"What? Why?"

"Because she said she didn't want to come between us. She asked about my face."

"And you told her?"

"I told her I said something to you that I shouldn't have."

"Great. She already thinks I'm a monster, but that's okay. I want her to hate me for what I've done."

"She doesn't think that, bro. She may hate you a little, but she doesn't think you're a monster. And why would you want her to hate you?"

"Because it'll be easier on both of us if she does."

He reached into his pocket and handed me a key.

"Julia asked me to give this back to you."

"Great." I shook my head as I clenched my fist. "Anyway, Dad wants to see us in his office."

"Dad? He's in today?"

"Yep. I'm just as shocked."

Stefan and I walked down to our father's office and opened the door.

"Boys, come in." He stood up from behind his desk, and when he saw our faces, a stern look crossed his face.

"You two were fighting?"

"It was just a misunderstanding," I said. "We're good."

"Welcome home, Dad," Stefan said.

"I didn't think you'd be in today. Your flight didn't get in until late last night," I said.

"I wanted to check on things. So, first things first. Sam, ask Julia to run the quarterly report. I have Joan working on something else at the moment."

Shit. I swallowed the hard lump in my throat.

"Dad, um, Julia doesn't work here anymore."

He cocked his head as a stern look crossed his face.

"Why not, Samuel?"

"She's opening her own coffee shop," Stefan jumped in.

"What?" He shook his head.

"Her former employer, Steven Hart, left her an empty building he purchased," I said.

"Okay. That came out of nowhere. So, she just up and quit."

Both of us sat there in silence.

"What the hell happened while I was gone?" he asked in a stern voice. "And don't try to bullshit me!"

"You want the bad news first or the really bad news first?" I asked.

"I said no bullshit, Sam."

"Ken Kramer pulled out of the company because Julia wouldn't sell him the building."

"Wait a minute. We lost the outdoor mall and the hospital?"

"Yep. I tried to get Julia to sell it to him because he threatened me if she didn't. We got into a huge fight, I said things I probably shouldn't have, she quit, and Ken took his business elsewhere."

"Stefan, I'll catch up with you later. I need to talk to your brother alone."

"Sure, Dad."

As soon as Stefan left his office, my dad paced around the room for a moment, and I braced myself for his wrath.

"Whatever you have to say to me, just say it. Because right now, anything you say to me will not hurt me anymore than I'm already hurting."

"You actually asked her to sell the building that Steven Hart left her so she could make something of herself and her life?" he asked.

"I did."

"Why, Sam? Why would you do that?"

"Because I was trying to save Ken Kramer's business with us. Do you realize how much money we've lost?"

"It's my fault. All my fault." He shook his head.

"What are you talking about?"

"You are putting business and this company before someone you care about."

"Dad—"

"Stop, Sam. I don't give two shits if Ken Kramer took his business elsewhere. There are plenty of projects and clients out there to keep us going for the rest of our lives. We're the best, and Ken will realize that he made a huge mistake one day. Why do you think I'm retiring already?"

"To travel?"

"To be with the woman I love very much. I've put this company first my whole life, and that's why all my marriages failed. I cared more about making as much money as possible instead of my family. And that is wrong on so many levels." He pointed at me. "I'm just sorry it took me this long to realize it. I've watched you and Julia together. You probably never noticed, but I was watching, and I saw something in your eyes that I'd never seen before. And I thought to myself. This is it. She's the one who's going to sweep my son off his feet, and he'll finally know what it's like to live for someone else. How much damage did you do with her?"

"A lot, Dad. A lot of damage." I looked down.

"The good thing about damage is it's always repairable."

"I don't think this damage can be repaired."

"All damage can be repaired, son. It just depends on how badly you want to fix it."

"I told her I didn't give a damn about her dreams."

"You were panicking because of Ken and his damn threat. That's understandable. We all make mistakes, son. God knows I've made more in my lifetime than I should have. But don't let that be the reason for giving up on someone. A wise man once told me that mistakes have the power to turn you into something better than you were before. I wish I would have listened to him years ago."

"Who told you that, Dad?"

"Your grandfather. So, I'm passing along that wisdom and praying that you'll listen to me."

"Thanks, Dad." I gave him a hug.

"You're welcome, son. And don't give Ken Kramer another thought. He's an asshole, and he'll regret what he did."

# CHAPTER 32

## ONE WEEK LATER

*Sam*

      I'd done something I never thought in a million years I'd do. I stalked Julia. Not in a creepy or scary way, however. I would park down the street of her shop just to catch a glimpse of her, and I'd go for a run in the mornings and make sure to pass her shop with the hopes I'd run into her. Which so far, hadn't happened, until today when I turned the corner, and I saw her struggling with the lock on the door.

"Julia."

She froze when she heard my voice and then slowly turned around.

"What are you doing here, Sam?"

"I was just going for a run, and I saw you standing here. Are you having problems with the lock?"

"No." She spoke with an attitude.

"It looked to me like you were. Let me see if I can get it."

"No."

"Julia, let me help you."

"I don't want or need your help, Sam. Just leave me alone." She turned around, stuck the key in the lock, and struggled with it.

"Damn it. What the hell is wrong with this thing?"

I reached out and placed my hand on hers, and she immediately dropped it. After fidgeting with the key, it finally unlocked the door.

"That lock needs to be replaced. I'll call a lock company and have them come out today."

"Don't bother. I'll call them myself," she spoke without looking at me.

"Julia, I—"

"I don't want to hear anything you have to say. Leave me alone, Sam," she scowled as she opened the door, stepped inside, and then locked it so I couldn't come in.

~

*J*ulia

My heart raced a million miles a minute, and it took me a few moments to catch my breath. I never expected to react as I did, but I couldn't help it. Seeing him again reminded me of the hurt he caused and the pain of his words. Feeling his hand touch mine sent tears to my eyes. It was nothing but a reminder of how much I once loved him.

Pulling up locksmiths in the area, I was lucky to find one that could come out within the hour. I took the paint samples I'd picked up from the paint store yesterday, and I taped them up on some of the walls to get a feel for which color I liked best. I needed to keep as busy as possible to keep my mind off him. Which was going to be difficult now that Jenni had left town again.

## ~

*S*am
      I went home, took a shower, changed into some fresh clothes, and headed to the office. I was late, but I didn't care. Seeing how she reacted towards me hurt, but I didn't blame her. It just confirmed that she wanted nothing to do with me ever again, and I would need to accept that.

When I arrived, I ran into Stefan, who was just leaving my office.

"There you are. Where have you been?" he asked.

"I went for a run this morning and ran into Julia."

"Oh. I'm afraid to ask how that went."

"It didn't go well." I sighed. "The lock on the door is bad, and it needs to be replaced. I told her that I'd call someone for her, and she said she'd do it herself. She wouldn't even look at me, Stefan. Her tone towards me was stone cold. She definitely hates me."

"Give it some time, Sam. It hasn't been that long. She needs to heal, and in time, she'll forgive you."

"I love you for what you're trying to do, but you don't know shit about relationships."

"I know, man. I'm sorry."

"It's okay. I think the best thing to do is forget about Julia Benton."

## ~

One Week Later

*J* was driving on the expressway when up ahead, there was a car pulled over on the side of the road that looked just like Julia's Jeep. I cut over a couple of lanes and pulled up behind her. I knew it was hers by the flower-shaped crystal she had hanging from her rearview mirror. Walking over to the passenger side, she rolled down the window and stared at me.

"Did your car break down?" I asked.

"No. I'm just sitting here on the side of the expressway collecting my thoughts because I have nothing better to do," she spoke in a sarcastic tone.

"Okay then. I thought you needed help. My bad. Have a good day." As I turned and headed back to my car, I smiled.

"Sam, wait!" she shouted as she climbed out of her car, and I stopped.

"My car did break down. It just started shaking, and when I pulled over, it went dead."

"Did you call someone?" I asked.

"No. I left my damn phone at the shop. I thought I put it in my purse."

"Would you like me to call a tow truck for you?"

"Please." She looked away from me.

I pulled out my phone and called Tony from Tony's Tow and gave him the location.

"Tony is sending a tow truck now. He said his guy will be here in about thirty minutes."

"You know him?"

"He's been a family friend for years. I'll wait with you until he gets here. Then I'll drive you to the shop to get your phone and then home."

"No. You go. I'm fine."

"And how are you getting back to the shop to get your phone? The tow truck will only take you as far as wherever you're having the car towed to."

"I'll call an Uber when I get there."

"You hate me that much to refuse a ride from me?" I asked with seriousness.

"Just leave me alone, Sam." She turned and went back to

her car.

I followed her and climbed into the passenger side before she had a chance to lock the door.

"Damn it, Sam."

"I'm staying, and then I'm driving you back. End of discussion, Julia. You can hate me all you want, but I will not leave you stranded on the side of the road alone."

"Whatever. But don't expect me to talk to you."

"That's fine. I won't expect anything, and I don't expect you to talk to me after everything I said to you. Which, by the way, I'm sorry."

"Save it, Sam. I don't want to hear it."

"I'm sorry I hurt you."

"What part of 'I don't want to hear it' do you not understand?" she yelled.

"Why, Julia? Because you're afraid that you'll forgive me?"

"I will never forgive you for what you said and did," she spoke through gritted teeth.

"Fair enough." I turned my head and looked out the window. "I miss you, Julia."

"La la la la." She placed her hands over her ears, and I sighed.

"Okay. That was childish," she spoke.

"Yes. It was." I smirked.

"Fine. You're sorry. Can you please stop talking now? We said everything we had to say that day."

"I said things I shouldn't have, and for that I'm—"

"No, Sam. You spoke exactly how you felt. Don't you have a personal assistant you need to get back to?"

"Nope. I put the brakes on that."

"Why?"

"Because nobody can replace you."

"Really? Because if I recall, you said I was replaceable."

"I didn't mean it. I was angry." I looked away from her out of shame.

The tow truck pulled up, so we climbed out of the car. As soon as he was done hooking up her car, we climbed in mine.

# CHAPTER 33

*J*ulia

Of course, he just happened to be driving by when I was broken down on the side of the road.

"I drank my coffee black this morning," he said. "I didn't have any cream."

"Good for you."

"I will admit, it wasn't bad."

"I told you," I spoke in a normal tone.

"You did, and I didn't listen. Just like I didn't listen to a lot of things you said. And for that, I'm sorry. How is Jenni doing?"

"She's out of town for a while for work."

"She's fierce, just like her sister."

"What do you mean?" I glanced over at him.

"The way she spoke to me that day when she came to collect your things. I thought she was going to rip my balls off." He smirked.

"What did she say?"

"She spoke her mind and then told me I had no soul."

"She said that?"

"Yes."

"She told me she didn't talk to you at all."

"And you believed her?" His brow arched. "She's your twin sister. Did you really think she would let what I'd done go? I know I wouldn't if it was one of my brothers."

He pulled up to the curb of my shop and put the car in park.

"Would you mind if I come in and take a look?" he asked.

"Suit yourself," I said as I got out of the car.

After unlocking the door, we stepped inside, and he looked around at the progress that was being made while I grabbed my phone.

"It's looking good. Stefan did an amazing job on designing this place."

"You can come clean, Sam. I know you're the one who did it."

"Why would you say that?"

"Because I paid attention to every little detail of all your designs. This is your work."

"Did you mention that to Stefan?"

"No. I didn't."

"I wanted to help, Julia."

"Why? You told me that you didn't give a damn about my coffee shop."

"I know what I said," I spoke out of frustration. "There's no need to rehash every statement that was made."

"Fair enough. Are you ready to go?"

"Yes. Just one small thing. We need to stop at my place quickly so I can change. I'm meeting my brothers for dinner. I promise it'll only take a few minutes."

"Fine. Let's go. I really want to get home."

It felt weird being in Sam's house again, where the pain and the hurt still filled the air. Walking around, I messed with his things. I couldn't help myself, and I stopped when I heard him coming down the stairs.

"I'm ready. I know this is last minute, but you're more than welcome to join us."

"Thanks, but I just want to go home."

"Okay. Then I'll take you home." A small smile crossed his lips.

When he pulled up to my building, I placed my hand on the doorhandle, and before I opened the door, I turned and looked at him.

"Thank you for helping me today."

"You're welcome. If you need anything, I want you to know you can always call me."

"I'd have to unblock your number first."

"I figured you'd done that since a couple of my text messages wouldn't go through."

"Thanks again. Enjoy your dinner with your brothers and tell them I said hi."

"I will. Have a nice evening, Julia."

I gave him a small smile and went inside the building. After starting the water for a bath, I twisted up my hair and climbed in to soak away the day's troubles. Spending a couple of hours with Sam was not how I planned my day. I did everything I could to avoid seeing him. But I did, and he was the man I'd first met in the Starlight Café. And he was the same man I'd officially met at the bar and the same man who became my boss. The man I fell in love with. But he had another side to him. A side I never wanted to see again. A businessman who only cared about money and nothing else. I needed to remember when that money was threatened, he turned into a totally different person. As I lay in the bubble-filled tub, I could feel the aching of my beating heart. The ache that was present not only because of him but because I let my wall down when I shouldn't have.

~

*S*am

I walked into Four Kinds and saw my brothers at our family table.

"You're late," Sebastian said.

"Sorry. I had to drive Julia home." The corners of my mouth curved upward.

"What?" Stefan looked at me with shock.

"I was driving down the expressway, and she was sitting in her car on the side of the road, broken down. So, I called a tow truck, drove her to her shop to get the phone she'd left there, and then drove her home."

"I'm afraid to ask how that went," Simon said.

"At first, it was a disaster, but we talked a little bit, and she was okay."

"You talked or yelled?" Stefan smirked.

"She yelled, I listened, and then she calmed down."

"So, does this mean the two of you are good again?" Sebastian asked.

"Further from it. But it's a start. A good start. By the way," I looked at Stefan, "she knows I'm the one who did the design."

"How?" His brows furrowed.

"She said when she worked for me, she paid attention to every little detail on all my designs, and she knew you didn't design it."

"She never told me that."

"And she won't either."

"Is she mad?"

"No. She's not mad. She's beautiful, and all I want is to see that sparkle in her eye again."

"I'm going to invite her to Lily's birthday beach bash."

"Do you think she'll come?" I asked.

"She'll come. Especially when I tell her Lily wants her there. She won't turn her down."

For the first time in a while, my heart wasn't aching, and my chest wasn't tight like it had been since Julia and I got into that fight. I tried to forget about her, but I couldn't. No matter what I did, she was always on my mind, and no matter how much I buried myself in my work, she was always there, first and forefront. After leaving the restaurant, I climbed into bed and stared up at the ceiling. Sleep hadn't been my friend since that day, and I was lucky if I even slept a few hours each night. Every time I closed my eyes, I saw her. When I'd roll over, the ache in my heart grew when my arm hit the empty side of the bed where she used to lay.

# CHAPTER 34

*J*ulia

I called an uber and had them drive me to the rental shop where a rental car was waiting for me. When I got to the shop, I walked in and set the three containers down I was carrying.

"Good morning." Stefan smiled.

"Good morning. I brought pastries for the guys, and coffee is on the way."

"You didn't have to do that."

"I wanted to. They've been working so hard."

"That was very sweet of you. Thank you. I have something for you." He handed me an envelope.

"What's this?" I smiled as I opened it. "An invitation to Lily's birthday?"

"Yeah. We both want you to come. She specifically told me you have to be there."

"She did?" My brow arched.

"She really likes you."

"And I really like her. Tell her I wouldn't miss it for the world." I grinned. "It must be tough raising her on your own."

"It's sometimes challenging, but Nanny Kate has been a godsend. If it wasn't for her, I don't know what I would have done."

"Can I ask a question?"

"Sure."

"Why does everyone call her Nanny Kate?"

He chuckled. "It's what she prefers. She said that's what all the families she used to nanny for called her over the years."

"It's cute. Anyway, I'm going to head to the lighting store to pick out the fixtures."

"Have fun. Thanks again for the pastries. I know the guys will love them."

"You're welcome. I'll talk to you later."

"Julia, wait."

I stopped and turned around.

"Sam told me about yesterday. He was in a really good mood."

"So was I when I messed with a few things of his while he was upstairs changing for dinner." I gave him a smirk.

"You're bad." He chuckled as he pointed at me. "I'm sure that gave you great pleasure."

"Oh, it did." I winked as I left the shop.

~

One Week Later

*W*hen I arrived at Stefan's house, I followed the noise of the screaming children to the back.

"Julia!" Lily ran up to me.

"Happy birthday, Lily." I knelt and hugged her.

"I'm so happy you came."

"I wouldn't have missed this birthday bash for the world. This is for you." I smiled as I handed her a wrapped gift.

"Thank you." She took my hand and led me over to where Stefan and Simon stood.

"Dad, look. Julia's here."

"Hi, Julia." He kissed my cheek.

"Hey, Julia. It's good to see you." Simon smiled as he kissed my other cheek.

"Good to see you, boys. Wow. You really went all out."

"I think Nanny Kate and I went a little overboard. But Lily is happy, and that's all that matters."

"There's a lot of moms here." I grinned.

"Yeah. When they said their kid was coming, they asked if they could stay. I guess they felt safer keeping an eye on their kid with the water and everything."

"Right." I nodded my head. "And you don't think it has anything to do with the fact that the four of you are here?" I arched my brow.

"The thought crossed my mind." He smirked.

"Can I get you a glass of wine or a beer?" Simon asked.

"A beer would be great."

He opened the cooler, took out a beer, popped off the cap, and handed it to me.

"Thanks, Simon."

As I brought the bottle to my lips, a handsome man walked up.

"Julia, I'd like you to meet my partner, Roman Burkes. Roman, this is my friend, Julia."

"It's nice to meet you, Julia."

"You too, Roman." I shook his hand.

Looking down at the beach, I saw Sam holding a beer and talking to an attractive woman. I pretended not to notice, but it was hard when my stomach felt like it had dropped a thousand feet. I turned around and saw Grayson walking over to me.

"Julia." He hugged me. "How are you?"

"I'm good, Grayson."

"We miss you at the office."

"I miss all of you too." I gave him a small smile.

"Stefan tells me the coffee shop construction is coming along nicely."

"It is. I hope when it's finished, you'll stop by. Coffee is on me."

"I definitely will."

"Hello, Julia." Sam walked up to me.

"I'll let the two of you talk. It's good seeing you again," Grayson spoke and walked away.

"Hi, Sam."

"Thanks for coming. I know it means a lot to Lily."

"Of course. I wouldn't miss the opportunity for a good party."

"How have you been?" he asked.

"Great. I got my car back yesterday."

"What was wrong with it?"

"They replaced the fuel pump."

"Ah."

There was an awkwardness between us. More so than last week.

"I was going to text you last week because the strangest thing happened. But I wasn't sure if you unblocked me or not."

"You're unblocked. What happened?"

"When I came home from Sebastian's restaurant that night, I noticed many things in the living room and kitchen were slightly moved." His lips formed a smirk.

"That's odd." I cocked my head.

"You just couldn't help it, could you?"

"No. I couldn't." I let out a laugh. "I'm sorry, but I'm not."

~

*S*am
     It was good to see and hear her laughter again.

"Sam, who is this lovely young lady?" my mother asked as she and her husband walked over to us.

"Mom, this is Julia. She used to work for me. Julia, this is my mother Barb and her husband, Curtis."

"It's nice to meet you both." Julia smiled.

"And you as well, Julia," my mother and Curtis both spoke. "So, what are you doing now that you no longer work at the company?" she asked.

"I'm in the process of opening a coffee shop on Sunset Blvd."

"How fun. What's it called?"

"Mojo Madness Café."

"What a fun name," Curtis said.

"Hello, son. Julia, it's good to see you again." My father hugged her. "Barb." He nodded. "Curtis." He extended his hand.

"Hello, Henry. Celeste." My mother looked Celeste up and down.

"Barb, you look lovely," Celeste said.

"I know I do, Celeste."

"Hey. I hate to break up the little party over here, but the food is ready," Stefan said.

"Good. I'm starving," my father said.

When both my parents and their spouses walked away, Julia started laughing.

"I know." I put my hand up. "Let's not even go there." I sighed.

We walked over to the large white canopy tent that was

set up with two eight-foot tables that were covered with different kinds of food. Hamburgers, hot dogs, Italian sausage, chicken kabobs, chicken fingers, a slew of different salads, French fries, sweet potato fries, potato chips. You name it, and Stefan provided it. Reece, one of the moms, walked over to me as we were going down the line and filling our plates.

"Hey, Sam. Would you like to join us at our table?"

"Thanks for the offer, but I'm sitting with Julia and my brothers."

"Oh." She looked Julia up and down. "Okay. Maybe next time." She walked away.

"You don't mind, do you? That woman has been following me around since I got here."

"I saw you talking to her when I came in."

"I couldn't get away from her fast enough. She told me her whole life story and then told me she hadn't had sex in months. Who just says that to a total stranger?"

"A horny mom who likes what she sees." She laughed.

# CHAPTER 35

ulia

The party had ended, and Sam walked over as I said goodbye to Stefan and Lily.

"You're leaving?"

"Yeah. I need to get home."

"I'll walk you to your car."

"No, Sam. It's okay. I'll see you around."

"Sure. Okay."

I climbed into my car and drove away. The last thing I needed was to be alone with him. The party was fine because there were a ton of people around all day, but I knew if the two of us were alone, there was no telling what would happen, even though I didn't want it to.

Walking into my apartment, I set down my purse, kicked off my shoes, and went to the kitchen for a glass of wine. After pouring some into a glass, I reached into my purse to grab my phone, and it wasn't there.

"Oh, come on," I said aloud as I frantically searched my purse.

Putting on my slippers and grabbing my keys, I went

down to where my car was parked and searched for my phone. It wasn't in there. I must have left it at Stefan's house.

"Shit!"

Running back up to my apartment, I slipped on my shoes, grabbed my purse, and when I opened the door, I saw Sam standing there.

"Looking for this?" The corners of his mouth curved upward as he held up my phone.

"Oh my God. I was panicking and just on my way back to Stefan's house. Um, come in."

"I saw it sitting on the table in the living room. You seem to be leaving your phone behind quite a bit."

"Yeah. I don't know what's wrong with me. Thank you for bringing it here. You didn't have to do that."

"I wanted to because I knew you'd be freaking out."

"Thanks." I stood in front of him and stared into his sexy eyes as my heart raced out of my chest.

"You're welcome," he spoke, bringing his hand to my cheek and softly stroking it.

The warmth of his touch paralyzed me, and I couldn't turn away. I swallowed hard as he leaned in and softly brushed his lips against mine. The tenderness of his kiss swallowed me up and like a fool, I kissed him back. He broke our kiss and pressed his forehead against mine.

"I'll go," he whispered.

I gave him a nod, and he turned and walked out the door. After locking it, I turned and slid my back down until I reached the floor as tears filled my eyes. I took in several deep breaths as I could feel the anxiety settling inside me.

Two Weeks Later

*S*am
    I hadn't seen or talked to Julia since that night. As many times as I picked up the phone to call her, I felt it best to leave her alone. She wasn't ready, and I finally realized that she might never be.

"Hey." Stefan opened the door and stepped inside. "Don't forget tonight we're celebrating Roman's birthday at the bar. Simon said we're to be there at seven-thirty."

"I'll be there. How's Julia?"

"She's fine."

"Has she asked about me?"

"No, bro. She hasn't."

"Okay. That's all the confirmation I need then."

"I'm sorry, Sam. Just give her some more time. She's been so busy with the shop. Between ordering the supplies and interviewing people, it's been crazy."

"Maybe," I said.

He left my office, and even though he was my brother, I resented him. I resented that he saw and talked to her every day while I struggled just to get through the day without her. Fuck that. I could feel the anger rise inside me. Enough was enough. Picking up my phone, I brought up Ashlyn's number and called her. After a few rings, it went to voicemail.

*"Ashlyn, it's Sam Kind. Hey, I'm attending a birthday party tonight at a bar and was wondering if you'd like to go with me? Give me a call and let me know. It's been a while."*

My phone rang about fifteen minutes later, and Ashlyn's name appeared.

"Hello, Ashlyn."

"Hey, Sam. You're right. It has been a while. I'd love to see you tonight. What time?"

"The party starts at seven-thirty. I can pick you up around seven."

"How about I meet you there? I don't get off work until six-thirty. I can be there by eight o'clock. Just text me the address."

"Sounds good. I'll see you later."

"What the hell are you doing?" Stefan asked as he walked back into my office.

"Are you eavesdropping now?"

"I was walking by, and I heard something I didn't like, so I stopped and listened to the rest of your conversation."

"What the fuck do you expect me to do, Stefan? I've waited long enough. It's obvious Julia is never going to fully forgive me."

"You don't know that! But whatever." He walked away.

~

*J* strolled into Pete's Bar and Grill at seven forty-five due to traffic being so backed up.

"It's about time you got here," Simon said.

"Traffic was a bitch due to an accident."

"Yeah. I heard about that over the scanner. Stefan told me you invited Ashlyn. What are you doing, bro?"

"What any other man would do after numerous rejections."

"Hey there, handsome. What can I bring you to drink?" Suzi, the head waitress, asked.

"Double scotch, Suzi."

"Coming right up."

Pete's bar and Grill was a bar that the L.A. cops frequently visited. Pete knew them all and was more than happy to accommodate them. He reserved one side of the bar for party guests only, while the other was for his regular patrons.

"Where's Sebastian?"

"Right here." He came up from behind, hooked his arm

around me, and pulled me into a neck hold. "What's this I hear about you inviting Ashlyn?"

"Do you want me to kick your ass?" I asked him. "You saw Stefan's face."

"And I also saw yours. You know damn well I can take you down."

"Okay, that's enough," Simon said. "Sebastian, let him go."

"Here you go, Sam." Suzi handed me my drink.

After wishing Roman a happy birthday, I talked to him and some of the guys and girls from the station. I'd almost forgotten I'd invited Ashlyn until she walked up and hooked her arm around me.

"Hey there, sexy."

"Hey." I kissed her cheek. "I'm glad you could make it."

"Me too. Thanks for the invite."

I looked over at my brothers, who stood there staring at me with disapproval in their eyes.

"Come on. Let's go over here." I led her to a table in the corner.

As I was talking to Ashlyn, I happened to look up and saw Julia and her sister walk in.

"Shit," I said.

"What?"

"Nothing. Hey, Suzi, I need another drink." I held up my glass.

She gave me a nod and headed to the bar. Stefan watched me and turned his head to see what I was staring at. Suddenly, his eyes widened, and he came running over.

"Ashlyn, you have to go," he said.

"What? Why?"

"Because we're all leaving and going over to the strip club. It's a surprise for Roman."

"Sam?" She turned and looked at me.

"Sorry, I didn't know."

"I can come. I don't mind strip clubs."

"Nope. You can't come," Stefan said as he basically took her from her seat. "No women allowed."

"But there are women cops here!" she shouted.

"They're going to do their own thing. We just met up for drinks. I'll escort you out."

"SAM!"

"Sorry, Ashlyn. As I said, I didn't know. I'll call you."

"Don't bother, asshole. In fact, lose my number because I'm blocking you!"

She stormed out of the bar, and I let out a deep breath.

"That was close," Stefan said. "Damn you for putting me in that position."

"What is she doing here? Did you know she was going to be here?"

"No! How would I know that? She doesn't fill me in on her personal life."

"Did you tell her we were coming here?"

"No. I didn't say a word about it. She's obviously having a night out with her sister."

"Bro, good job. I saw that." Sebastian high-fived him, and I kept my eyes focused on Julia.

I picked up the glass of scotch Suzi set down and brought it up to my lips as I carefully watched two douchey-looking guys walk up to the bar and start chatting with Julia and Jenni.

# CHAPTER 36

*S*am

The look on her face. She had the same smile plastered across it as she did the night I met her at the bar. I could feel the rage inside me fighting to get out.

"Don't even think about it, Sam," Simon said as he sat down next to me. "This is a bar full of cops. Don't do anything stupid."

"I can't guarantee that, Simon."

I sat back in my chair while I sipped my scotch and watched. The man was getting a little too cozy for my liking, and she seemed to be enjoying it.

"That's it." I pushed myself up from my seat and headed over there.

"Shit." I heard Simon say.

"Excuse me." I tapped him on the shoulder. "She's with me."

"Sam! What are you doing here?"

"I need to talk to you."

"Who do you think you are just interrupting our conversation like that?" the guy spoke. "Fuck off, dude."

I grabbed him by the collar of his shirt and pulled him closer to me.

"I will bury you six feet under if you don't get the fuck out of my way," I spoke through gritted teeth.

"Okay. Okay. Damn man. Chill out." He walked away.

"What the hell do you think you're doing?" she asked angrily.

"The question is, what the hell do you think you're doing?"

"Sam, leave her alone," Jenni intervened.

"Jenni, I can handle this. I'm having a few drinks with my sister who just returned home. How dare you do what you just did!"

"How dare me? How dare you let some random guy talk you up like that."

"Excuse me?! You have no right, Samuel Kind!"

~

*J*ulia

"I have every right to keep you safe," he spoke through gritted teeth.

"I'm not listening to this. I need some fresh air."

I grabbed my purse and headed out of the bar. Before I knew it, Sam grabbed hold of my arm and spun me around.

"Will you just fucking talk to me?" he spat.

I stared at him with wide eyes as his grip around my arm loosened.

"I can't," I spoke calmly.

"Why, Julia?"

"Because I'm afraid if I do, I'll forgive you, and I don't want to forgive you." Tears filled my eyes as I turned away from him.

"It all makes sense now," he said. "You're afraid if you forgive me, I'll hurt you again. You're protecting yourself."

"I have never felt so used by someone like I did you in my entire life."

He wrapped his arms around me from behind and held me. The more I struggled to get out from under him, the more his grip tightened.

"I will never hurt you again. I promise you that," he whispered in my ear.

"I'm broken, Sam."

"Then let me put you back together. Let me fix what I broke."

"Get a room," Someone yelled as they walked by us, and we both started to laugh.

"Let me take you back to my place, and we can talk. Just talk—nothing else. I promise. Then after, I'll drive you home."

"I just can't leave Jenni in there by herself."

"Okay. Then let's go back inside."

I nodded my head, and he let go of me. When we stepped inside the bar, I saw Jenni chatting it up with Sam's brothers and the other guys there.

"She seems to be having a good time," Sam said.

"Yeah. She does. I'll go tell her I'm leaving with you."

"And I'll tell my brothers to keep an eye on her."

Walking up to Jenni, I tapped her on the shoulder.

"Oh, hey." She grinned. "Are you okay?"

"Do you mind if I leave with Sam? We have some talking to do."

"Not at all. You go ahead and work out your issues. I'm just going to hang back here and party it up with the guys."

"I'm warning you right now, Jennifer Mae. You are not to sleep with any of Sam's brothers. Understand me?"

"But they're so hot." She whined.

195

"Understand me?" I spoke in an authoritative tone.

"Fine. I won't."

"You can have any other guy in this place. Just not the three of them."

"Okay. Okay. You've made your point."

"Are you ready?" Sam walked up and asked.

"Yes. I'm ready."

We climbed in his car, and he drove us to his house. When we stepped inside, I set my purse down, and he went into the kitchen and poured me a glass of wine.

"Here you go."

I took the glass from his hand.

"Thank you. Sam—"

"Julia—"

We both spoke at the same time.

"You, first." Sam smiled.

"You were right when you said that I was protecting myself. I am. I've gone back behind the shell I had around me before I met you. Avoidance of Loss. That's what my therapist calls it. I'm so afraid of losing someone I love again that I spent the last four years avoiding any emotional connection with a man. Then I met you. And little by little, you cracked through that hard exterior surrounding me. I let myself feel again, and once it started, I couldn't stop it. And god knows how I tried so hard to." Tears filled my eyes. "The day we fought, it was my wake-up call. The voice inside my head kept saying, 'you stupid, stupid girl.'"

"Julia, I swear on my life that I didn't mean anything I said. I was scared too because I'd never had feelings for anyone like I have for you. My whole life had been one revolving door between my parents and their multiple spouses. When one would leave, another would come in. The only stability I have in life is my brothers. When my father left us, he did it because he wanted to pursue his dream of creating the biggest and best architect firm in the country. I guess I was afraid if you followed your dream, you'd leave me too."

"You said the things you did because of what Ken threatened," I said.

"He was only part of the reason, Julia. Not the whole reason. My father told me that making a mistake has the power to change you into something better than you were before. I made a mistake with you, which really opened my eyes to what I lost. And now, because of that, I feel like I'm a better man than I was before I met you. I love you, Julia, and I want to be with you. I want to share my life with you, and I want you to share your life with me. It's been killing me that I haven't been able to be a part of helping you create your dream coffee shop."

"You designed the inside."

"But I wanted to be there every step of the way. I know I'm not Justin, but I sure as hell want to be the man he was to you."

"Ouch," I said.

"What's wrong?"

"I think you just cracked through my shell again." I gave him a small smile as I watched the corners of his mouth curve upward.

He walked over to where I stood, wrapped his arms around me, and held me tight.

"I will break through that entire shell and smash it into a million little pieces."

"Promise?" I asked in a soft voice as I melted in his arms.

He broke our embrace and held my face in his hands.

"I promise." His lips softly brushed against mine.

# CHAPTER 37

*S*am
  As I slowly thrust in and out of her, I stared into her eyes as she took in the pleasure. The softness of her moans heightened my arousal as her nails dug into the flesh of my skin. I wanted this moment to last forever, but I couldn't hold back anymore, and I exploded inside her. Dropping my body on hers, we held onto each other as if it was the end of the world. This moment was the beginning of the rest of my life.

"I love you," I whispered in her ear.

"I love you too," her soft voice spoke.

Rolling onto my back, I pulled her into me, for I would never let this woman go again.

"I've missed this," she spoke as her finger trailed across my chest.

"Me too. More than you'll ever know."

The next morning, I woke up with a smile as my arm was wrapped tightly around her. Pressing my lips to the back of her head, she stirred and rolled over.

"I didn't mean to wake you."

"I'm happy you did." A beautiful smile graced her face.

"What are your plans for today?" I asked.

"Spending the day with you."

"I was hoping you'd say that." I kissed the top of her head.

Suddenly, my phone pinged, and when I grabbed it from the nightstand, there was a message from Sebastian in our group chat.

*"Waves. Twenty minutes."*

"Let me guess. Surfing?" she asked.

"Yeah. But I don't have to go. I'd much rather stay in bed with you all day."

"Nope." She sat up. "You're going. So, get up, get ready, and I'll make coffee before you head out."

"Are you sure?"

"I'm positive. We have all day." She pressed her lips against mine.

~

*J*ulia

I slipped into one of his t-shirts and walked down to the kitchen to make our coffee. Opening the refrigerator, I went to grab the creamer, and there wasn't any. Shit.

"Hey, did you know you're out of creamer?" I asked as he walked into the kitchen.

"I do." The corners of his mouth curved upward. "I don't use it anymore."

"What?" I grinned.

"You've turned me over to the dark side." His hand cupped my chin.

"For real? Or are you messing with me?"

"No. For real. After I tried it without the creamer, I liked it. So, I stopped buying it and got used to drinking it black." He kissed my forehead. "I won't be long."

"Enjoy the waves," I said as I watched him walk out the sliding door and grab his surfboard.

As I took my coffee outside and watched Sam and his brothers put their boards in the water, something out of the corner of my eye caught my attention. Looking over, I saw Jenni waving as she walked towards the house while I gave her a look of disapproval.

"Come on. You promised me."

"You can blame it on the alcohol. I had nothing to do with it." She grinned.

"Which one?"

"Simon. He couldn't wait to show me his gun, and I couldn't wait to see it."

"Ugh, Jenni."

"Stop. It was a one-night stand for both of us."

"I take it you and Sam worked things out?"

"We did." I smiled as I brought the cup up to my lips and stared out at him as he surfed. "He told me he loves me."

"I'm so happy for you, sis." She hooked her arm around me.

"Want some breakfast?"

"As much as I'd love to stick around, I'm going to head home, shower, and meet Trina for lunch. I'll talk to you later."

"Okay." I gave her a hug.

"I'm really happy for you, sis."

After she left, I went inside and walked up the stairs to climb back into bed so I could look for some décor for the shop while Sam was surfing. When I reached the bedroom, I stood in the doorway and shook my head while staring at the perfectly made bed. Sighing, I went into the bathroom and started the shower. As the hot water streamed down my back, the shower door opened, and Sam stepped inside. Gripping my hips, he softly kissed my lips.

"How was your surf?"

"It was good. A lot of waves this morning."

"Why are you taking a shower already?" he asked.

"Well, I came up here to climb back in bed and found it was already made."

"Oh." He let out a chuckle. "Sorry about that."

"No, you're not." I laughed.

"You're right. I'm not." He pulled me into him, and the feeling of his hard cock against me sent shivers down my spine. "Now give me those lips."

❧

*S*am took me home so I could change my clothes and pack a bag for a few days' stay at his house. When we walked into my bedroom, I cringed when I saw my unmade bed. He stared at it and then glanced over at me with an arch in his brow.

"You never made your bed yesterday?"

"I guess I forgot." I walked over to the closet, grabbed my bag, and started packing.

I heard him sigh as he walked over and began making it.

"You really don't have to do that," I said.

"Oh, but I do, Julia. My goal is to get you to make the bed the minute you get out of it."

"Never." I smiled at him.

"Never say never, my love. I will train you, young Jedi," he spoke in a husky voice.

"Don't do that again." I waved my finger at him.

"Yeah. That was pretty bad." He laughed.

When we left my apartment, we headed to the coffee shop. After unlocking the door, we stepped inside, and satisfaction and warmth flowed through me. Two of the walls were covered in a light gray brick which enhanced the black-framed floor-to-ceiling windows that let in the natural light. Whitewashed oak flooring covered the entire place with small light oak tables and black chairs that sat upon it. Swirling globe glass pendant lights with warm-colored bulbs hung from the ceiling that gave off cozy vibes. Over by the stage, two black sofas sat across from each other with a chic coffee table in between. Glass cases for pastries graced the front, and a long coffee bar and bar stools extended from the ordering area where people could also sit and enjoy a cup of magic.

"This looks incredible." Sam smiled as he hooked his arm around me.

"You really like it?"

"I love it. You have done an amazing job decorating this place. It's going to be the hottest spot around. I can see it now. People will be lined up down the boulevard to get into this place."

"You're being dramatic."

"I'm serious, Julia. I can feel it."

"I'm still waiting on the fence people to put up the small black wrought iron fence outside, and I'm still waiting on the outdoor furniture. I also need to get some more greenery. With any luck, I'll be able to open the doors within a month or two."

"Stefan told me you're interviewing people."

"I am. Jasper is coming to work as my manager, and I've hired six additional people already. They are all very quali-fied baristas, and they have great personalities. I want to create a family atmosphere with the employees. I'm going to do right by them and give them incentives to do the best job they can do. We'll have an employee of the month, bonuses, employee appreciation parties, and a few other things."

"Wow. You sound like a dream boss. Can I come work for you?" He grinned.

"I know you're super busy with your job, but I'm hoping you'll be a big part of this café."

"I wouldn't have it any other way. And I will always make time for you and this place. Anything you need, ask, and it's yours." He pulled me into him.

"Have I told you how much I love you?" I looked up at him.

"Not since this morning." A smirk crossed his lips.

"I love you, Sam Kind."

"I love you, too, my love."

As our lips tangled with passion, the door opened, and my parents walked in.

"Oh my. Are we interrupting?"

"Mom! Dad! What are you doing here?" I asked in shock.

"We were driving by, and we saw the lights on. So, we parked the car and took our chances that you were here," my dad spoke.

"If we're interrupting, we can come back another time." My mother grinned.

"It's nice to see you again, Mr. & Mrs. Benton." Sam smiled as he held out his hand.

"Mom. Dad. You remember Sam."

"Of course. How could we forget such a handsome face," my mom spoke as she placed her hand on Sam's cheek.

*I wanted to die.*

"Am I to assume that the two of you are dating?" my dad asked.

"We are. I love your daughter very much, and I plan on making her the happiest woman alive."

"Oh." My mom placed her hand over her heart. "Julia Marie. Why didn't you say anything to us?"

"I was going to, Mom. But I've been so busy with this place. Let me show you around."

After showing my parents around the shop and talking for a while, they left.

"You didn't tell them what happ—"

"God, no. The only thing they know is that I quit working for you to work on the shop."

"Phew. I was nervous there for a minute. But I wouldn't blame you if you did."

"They only know what I want them to know." I reached up and kissed his mouth.

# CHAPTER 38

## ONE MONTH LATER

*Sam*

Julia and I spent every night together either at her place or mine. The last thing I wanted to do was put more pressure on her with the opening of Mojo Madness in a couple of weeks, but I didn't want to wait any longer. I was lying in bed when she emerged from the bathroom, climbed on the bed, and sat up Indian style facing me.

"Okay. So, I need to go over everything with you for the shop's opening. I need you to tell me if I miss anything because this is very important, and I can't screw this up. Oh my God, what if something goes wrong and I embarrass myself? What if I didn't order enough beans or supplies? Shit. I'm starting to second-guess myself. Do you think I'm over-thinking it?"

I stared at her with a smile on my face.

"What? Why aren't you answering me?"

"Move in with me."

"What?"

"You heard me. I want you to move in with me."

"As in live here?" she cocked her head.

"Yes." I chuckled. "Isn't that what moving in means?"

"Oh my God. Yes." She threw her arms around me. "When?"

"The sooner, the better. The shop is five minutes from here. It'll be easier for you, and it'll be easier for me."

"How will it be easier for you?"

"We'll stop packing bags and traveling between two places."

"Ah. That sounds like a dream." She grinned.

"We both know dreams come true." I kissed the tip of her nose.

"I'd love to move in with you, Sam, but one question."

"Yes, Julia. If you're the last one out of bed, you'll have to make it the minute you get up."

Her brows furrowed.

"I wasn't going to ask that."

"Yes, you were."

"You're a jerk."

"I'm your jerk, and that's all that matters. Enough talk. We have some celebrating to do." I rolled her on her back and hovered over her.

～

Two Weeks Later

*J*ulia

It was the day before I opened the doors to my coffee shop, and I was a nervous wreck. My staff had been working like crazy the past couple of weeks to help get it ready, and I couldn't have been more grateful. The day after Sam asked me to move in with him, I spent the day with Jenni and broke the news to her. She was sad but thrilled at the same time. Her friend Trina had just broken up with her boyfriend and since he refused to move out of their apartment, she needed a place of her own. So, Jenni asked her to move in which made me feel a lot better about moving out. Within a few days, Sam and I packed my things and brought them to his house.

"Calm down, Julia," Jasper said as he gripped my shoulders. "Everything is perfect. There's nothing to worry about."

"I can't help it."

The door to the shop opened, and a delivery man walked in holding a large box.

"Flowers for Julia Benton," he said.

"That's me." I smiled.

"I just need you to sign here."

After signing for the flowers, I took them over to the counter and unwrapped them. It was a beautiful white vase filled with different kinds of exotic flowers with roses mixed in. Opening the small envelope, I removed the card inside.

*Congratulations on making your dreams come true, my love. I love you so much, and I will always stand by your side.*
*Love forever,*
*Sam*

Tears filled my eyes as I looked at Jasper.

"That man is one of a kind. You're so lucky to have him, Julia."

"I know." I began to cry.

"Tears of joy, sweetheart. Tears of joy." He hugged me.

After I composed myself, I called Sam.

"Hello, beautiful."

"Hi. Thank you for the flowers. They're gorgeous."

"You're welcome. As much as I don't want to hang up, I have a meeting to get to with Stefan."

"That's okay. I'll see you later."

"Before we hang up, did you make the bed this morning? You were still sleeping when I left."

"Of course, I did. You've trained me well."

After I ended the call, I grabbed my purse.

"Where are you going?" Jasper asked.

"I forgot to make the damn bed. I'll be right back. Thank God, I'm close." I flew out the door.

I arrived at the house, slid the key in the lock, and ran upstairs. When I reached the bedroom, I jumped when I saw Sam sitting on the edge of the bed with a smile on his face.

"Jesus. What are you doing here? I thought you were at work."

"I was. I just stopped by to change my shirt. There's a hole in it that I didn't notice."

"I didn't see your car out there."

"It's in the garage." He smirked.

"Oh. You set me up." I pointed as I slowly walked towards him.

"And you lied to me."

"Please. I don't consider that a lie. You would never have known if you hadn't come home, and it wouldn't have been a lie."

He wrapped his arms around my waist as I stood in front of him.

"Now I'm going to have to punish you."

"Promise." I smiled as I sat down on his lap.

"I'm going to spend the day thinking about it, and you better be ready for me when I get home." His lips brushed against mine.

"Okay. Sounds like a plan." I jumped up from his lap. "Get

your ass off the bed so I can make it. I have to get back to the shop. Chop. Chop." I clapped my hands.

"Damn." He grinned as he stood up. "I think I like this bossy side of you." His lips pressed against my neck. "I'll see you later, babe."

# CHAPTER 39

*J*ulia

It was opening day for Mojo Madness, and the shop was filled with family, friends, and locals who came in to check out the place. Although I'd had extreme anxiety leading up to this day, I was impressed at how calm I was.

To get people in the door, I offered free coffee and pastries as a perk for stopping by. I had my back turned behind the counter when I heard the shop go silent, and Sam started speaking. Turning around, I saw him sitting on the stool on the small stage, holding his guitar.

"I've never been prouder of anyone than I am right now of the beautiful woman who owns this coffee shop. This is for you, baby."

I stepped out from behind the counter as he strummed his guitar and started singing, *Can't Nobody Love You* by Solomon Burke. I walked over and took a seat on the soft as his eyes stared into mine throughout the entire song. When he strummed the last chord, everyone started clapping and shouting. Getting up from the sofa, I took a seat on his lap.

"That was beautiful." He wiped the tears from my face. "I can't believe you sang in public like that."

"I'd do anything for you. You should know that by now. I'm so proud of you, Julia. All your hard work has paid off. Look at this place. It's packed."

"I love you so much, Sam. I couldn't have finished it without you and your support."

"Excuse me," Stefan said. "What about me? Huh? I think I played a huge part in this." He smiled.

I got up from Sam's lap and threw my arms around him.

"Thank you, Stefan. You did an amazing job."

"I helped too," Sebastian said. "I hooked you up with some wholesalers."

I smiled as I hugged him. "Thank you. Without your help, I wouldn't have saved the money I did."

"I'm bringing in all my cop buddies, and this is going to become their new favorite spot. You will always be protected here," Simon said.

"Thank you, Simon." I hugged him.

~

*S*am
    I stood up from the stool and shook my head. My brothers. They would say anything to get a hug from a beautiful woman.

"Nice job with the song, son." My father walked over and extended his hand. "You had Celeste in tears."

"Thanks, Dad."

"Julia did a wonderful job here. I always knew that girl had something special."

"Yeah. She is special."

"I'm happy to see that spark in both your eyes again. Just

remember, your woman always takes priority over everything else."

"I know, Dad. Trust me."

"Now, we need to get that spark in your brother's eyes."

"I don't think that's happening anytime soon."

"We'll see. Anyway, Celeste and I are going to head home. I'm going to say goodbye to Julia. You know, it would be nice to have a daughter in the family." He gave me a wink before walking away.

He didn't know that I already had planned on asking Julia to marry me. I just need it to be the perfect moment once everything with the shop settles down.

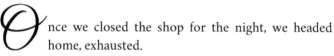

$\mathcal{O}$nce we closed the shop for the night, we headed home, exhausted.

"I'll pour us some wine," I said.

"Okay. Let's drink it out on the beach. I'll grab a blanket and meet you down there."

"Sounds good."

After I poured us each a glass, I took it down to the beach and sat next to her on the blanket.

"To new beginnings." I held up my glass.

"To new beginnings." She tapped her glass against mine.

"I can't help but feel a little scared, Sam."

"Scared about what?"

"What if the shop doesn't make it?"

"Are you kidding? Did you see all the people there today who weren't family and friends?"

"Yeah. But remember, I was offering free coffee and pastries. You know how people love free stuff."

"And I'm sure they loved it, and they'll be back. It's going to do very well, Julia. Steven wouldn't have given you your dream if he didn't think you couldn't make it happen. He believed in you as much as I do."

"Thank you." She laid her head on my shoulder, and I pressed my lips against it.

"Are we interrupting?" I heard Stefan's voice.

Turning around, all three of my brothers walked towards us with a bottle of wine and glasses in their hands.

"I guess not." I sighed.

"Yeah. I didn't think so," Simon messed up my hair before sitting down next to me.

"Sorry, Julia. But when you have one brother, you have us all." Sebastian grinned.

# CHAPTER 40

## THREE MONTHS LATER

*J*ulia

The coffee shop was doing better than I had ever imagined. Every morning, people were lined up at the door waiting for their morning fix on their way to work. Every afternoon, the place was packed with people sitting down, either scrolling through their phones, working on their laptops, or just enjoying the coziness of a good book. I was incredibly proud of the staff I hired, and they were already like family. Not just to me, but to each other as well.

I was helping a customer at the register when I saw Sam walk in, and the smile on my face grew wider.

"May I help you, sir?" I gave him a smirk as he walked up to the counter.

"I was passing by and saw the goods in this place. I was hoping you'd let me sample something first."

"What would you like to sample?"

"I need you to come closer so nobody else will hear."

Leaning over the counter, he whispered in my ear.

"Oh my God." I slapped his arm. "You are so bad."

"You love it when I'm bad." He kissed my lips. "Anyway, make me one of those amazing macchiatos you do so well." He grinned.

"Coming right up."

"You're still leaving the shop by seven, right?" he asked.

"Yeah. Why?"

"I thought we could have dinner down by the beach. I could pick something up, and we'd spread out a blanket and enjoy a nice evening by the water."

"Sounds like a dream date. I'm in. I'll be home at 7:10 at the latest." I handed him his macchiato.

"Thanks, baby. I'll see you tonight."

"I want a boyfriend like that someday," Michelle, one of my employees, swooned as she watched Sam leave the shop.

"You'll find one. It took me four years to find that man." I glanced over at her with a smile.

~

*I* said goodbye to my employees and left the shop at 7:00 pm like I promised Sam I would. When I walked into the house, I set my purse down and went into the kitchen, where I found a note from Sam lying on the counter.

*Down at the beach. I laid out a dress for you. Once you get changed, meet me down there. I'll be waiting. By the way, you really need to clean your closet.*
*Love forever,*
*Sam*

I let out a laugh and went upstairs. I couldn't figure out why I had to wear a dress. Picking up the black dress laid out on the bed, I slipped into it. But there was no way I was wearing heels in the sand, so I opted to go barefoot.

When I opened the sliding door and looked down at the beach, I saw a white tent glowing with white string lights and a table for two. Walking towards it with a smile on my face, Sam turned around in his black tuxedo.

"What is going on?" I walked up and wrapped my arms around his waist. "Why are we so fancy?"

"We've both been so busy with work lately that we really haven't had a chance to go somewhere special. So, I thought I'd bring the special to you, where it's just the two of us."

"You are so amazing." I reached up and kissed his lips.

"Your seat, madame." He gestured as he walked over and pulled out the chair for me.

"Thank you." I sat down.

He took the seat across from me, and suddenly, Sebastian walked over holding a tray with two glasses of champagne on it.

"Oh my gosh. What is all this?" I grinned.

"Sebastian agreed to cook for us tonight," Sam spoke.

"That is so nice of you." I placed my hand on Sebastian's arm. "Thank you."

"You're welcome. Dinner will be served in a couple of minutes.

"I can't believe you did all this." I reached over and placed my hand on Sam's.

"I did it for you. You've been working so hard at the shop, and you deserve to have something special done for you."

We started dinner off with a Caesar salad and homemade bread. When we were finished, Sebastian walked over, set our plates down, and removed the lids.

"OH! Is this—"

"Asparagus and lemon ricotta stuffed salmon with a

lemon sauce," Sebastian spoke. "With a side of roasted herb redskins."

"My absolute favorite!" I exclaimed. "What did I do to deserve this?" I asked Sam. "Is it because of what I did the other night?" I smiled. "Because if that's the reason, I will do it more often."

"Whoa, Julia. Stop with the dirty talk. You're turning me on. I did this because you're you. Plain and simple."

"I love you, Sam."

"I love you, too. Let's eat, shall we?"

We talked about our day while devouring the delicious dinner Sebastian prepared for us. When we finished, Sebastian walked over and handed Sam his guitar.

"What are you doing?" I smiled.

"Serenading you." He strummed a few chords. "I hope you like it."

He strummed the melody and began singing "Marry Me" by Train. Tears filled my eyes as I brought my hands up to my face. Was he doing what I thought he was? I swallowed hard to keep the tears from falling while I sat and listened to him. He got up from his seat and knelt before me as he strummed the last chord. Setting his guitar down, he pulled a small box from his pocket and flipped open the lid.

"Will you marry me, Julia?" He slipped the most beautiful diamond ring on my finger.

"Yes, Sam! Yes! I will marry you." I jumped up from my chair as he stood up, threw my arms around his neck, and smashed my mouth into his.

"I love you so much, Julia. I can't imagine spending the rest of my life without you."

"I love you, Sam."

Suddenly, all three of his brothers started clapping and shouting as they walked towards us. Lily came running up and hugged me.

"You're going to be my aunt, and that makes me so happy."

"And you're going to be my niece. And since you're practically an adult, I'd love for you to be my junior bridesmaid." I smiled as I tapped her on the nose.

"Did you hear that, Dad? I'm going to be a junior bridesmaid."

"I heard, princess. That's so awesome."

His brothers took their turns hugging and congratulating us. I was still in shock because we had never discussed marriage before.

"I think this calls for a dance," Sam said as he pulled a small black remote out of his pocket and pushed a button. Suddenly, the song, *Cry to Me* started playing. The same song we danced to for the first time in Montauk.

The six of us danced together in the sand that night as I became a permanent part of their family—the future Mrs. Julia Kind.

## CHAPTER 41

### ONE WEEK LATER

*J*ulia

"I'm heading out, babe." Sam walked into the kitchen and kissed me goodbye. "I love you."

"I love you too. I'll see you later."

Fifteen minutes later, after changing my shirt because I had spilled coffee on it, I ran to the kitchen to grab my purse, and I heard Lily screaming from her house. Grabbing my phone, I flew out the door and ran to the back of Stefan's house, where I knew the sliding door would be open.

"Lily!" I screamed.

"In here, Julia."

I ran into the living room and found Nanny Kate lying on the floor.

"Oh my God." I ran over to check her pulse. "Lily, what happened?"

"She just fell to the ground," she cried hysterically.

"Can you dial 911 for me and put it on speaker?"

She took my phone and did exactly as I asked. After giving the operator all the information, she told me an ambulance was on the way.

"Is she going to be okay?" Lily asked.

"I'm fine," Nanny Kate spoke as she started to come to, and Lily grabbed her hand.

She went to get up and immediately laid back down.

"Just stay put. The ambulance is on their way," I said.

I heard sirens, and when I opened the front door, Simon came running up with the paramedics.

"Julia, what happened? Is Lily okay? I heard the call over the scanner, and when they gave this address, I freaked the fuck out."

"She's fine. It's Nanny Kate. She passed out."

He ran into the living room, and I grabbed Lily and held her against me.

"Are they taking her to the hospital?" she asked.

"Yes, baby. The doctors are going to check her out and make sure she's okay."

"I want to go."

"I'll call Stefan, tell him what happened and that we'll meet him at the hospital. You and Lily can ride in my car. I can get us there faster."

"Okay. I just have to run home and grab my purse."

When we stepped inside the ER, Stefan wasn't there yet. Simon went up to the desk to see if he could find out any information. Pulling my phone from my purse, I had six missed calls from Sam. Just as I was about to call him, he and Stefan walked into the ER.

"Daddy!" Lily yelled as she ran to him. He immediately picked her up and held her tight.

"Are you okay?" Sam walked up and hugged me.

"I'm fine."

"What the hell happened?" Stefan asked.

"I was getting ready to leave for work, and I heard Lily screaming, so I ran over there, and that's when I found Nanny Kate on the floor."

"Why didn't you answer my calls?" Sam asked.

"Because I didn't hear my phone ring. I'm sorry."

His grip around me tightened.

"Sam, I thought she was—"

"I know, baby." His lips pressed against the side of my head. "Thank God you were still home. Lily had to be scared to death."

"She was."

"The doctors are in with her now." Simon walked over to us. "One person can go back and be with her."

"Come on, Lily." Sam held out his arms to her. "Let your dad go see how Nanny Kate is doing."

"But I want to go!" she whined.

"You can't, princess. Only grown-ups are allowed back there."

"I can bring her to the shop with me," I said. "Hey, Lily, do you want to come to the shop with me, and I'll teach you how to make coffee?"

"Yeah." Her eyes lit up.

"Thank you, Julia." Stefan hugged me.

Sam set Lily down, and I took hold of her hand.

"We rode with Simon in his car. Can you drive us home so I can get mine?"

"Of course." He hooked his arm around me.

~

One Week Later

*S*am

  I was sitting behind my desk when Stefan opened the door and walked into my office.

"Hey, bro. How's Nanny Kate doing?"

"It's not good, Sam." He lowered his head and took a seat

across from my desk. "She has stage three pancreatic cancer."

"Oh my God, Stefan. I'm so sorry." I got up from my desk, walked over to where he sat, and hugged him.

"Her sister lives in Maryland, and her nephew is a doctor at John Hopkins. They have a top-notch specialist there he's getting her in to see. So, she's moving there and living with her sister. Which is for the best because she's a nurse."

"Shit. I'm sorry. Does Lily know?"

"I sat her down this morning and told her."

"I'm sure she didn't take it well."

"Not at all. She cried hysterically. She loves her. Damn it, Sam. I don't want her to be sick like this, and I don't want her to leave. What am I going to do?"

"You're going to raise your daughter the best way you know how. We're here for you, bro. You have me, Julia, Mom, Dad, Sebastian, and Simon. We'll all help. You know that. When is she leaving?"

"Her flight leaves tomorrow morning."

"Take as much time off as you need. I'll handle everything. In the meantime, it might not be a bad idea to look for someone else to help out."

"Nanny Kate is all Lily has ever known. I'm not sure how well she is going to take to another person."

"It might be tough at first, but she'll adjust. Children are resilient. Look at us."

"Really, Sam?"

"Okay. Maybe not a great example. But Lily is a well-rounded, smart little girl, and she'll be okay. I'll have Julia talk to her. She's dealt with loss. Maybe she can give her some guidance."

"Yeah. Maybe. I have to go."

"I'm here for you, Stefan. We all are." I gave him a hug.

As I was getting ready to leave for the day, Grayson stepped into my office.

"You wanted to see me, Sam?"

"Yeah. I think Stefan is going to take some time off due to the Nanny Kate situation, and I'm going to oversee the building division. So, I need you to work on finding me a personal assistant."

"Okay." He nodded his head. "Anything you don't want?" His brow raised.

"I'm getting married, Grayson. It doesn't matter. As long as she's good."

"I'll get on it first thing tomorrow morning."

"Thanks." I smiled at him.

I climbed into my car and headed to the café. Julia had her back turned when I walked in, so I stepped behind the counter and wrapped my arms around her.

"Not here. What if my fiancé happens to walk in?"

"I'll tell him how in love I am with you and how you're mine and only mine."

She turned around and wrapped her arms around my neck.

"Then maybe we should run away together." The corners of her mouth curved upward.

"Anywhere you want to go is fine with me. Just say the word." I brushed my lips against hers. "Are you ready to go home?"

"Yes." She flashed a beautiful smile as she ran her finger down my chest. "Why don't you go home, pour us a glass of wine, and start the water for a bath. I'll be right behind you."

"That sounds like an excellent idea. I'll see you in a few." I softly kissed her lips.

"Make sure you turn the jets on high," she said before I walked out of the shop.

"I was already planning on it." I gave her a wink.

# CHAPTER 42

*J*ulia

"Jasper, I'm leaving for the night."

"Enjoy your evening, Julia. I'll see you tomorrow."

When I got home, I set my purse down and ran up the stairs to my future husband. Walking into the bathroom, I smiled when I saw him lying in the tub holding a glass of wine.

"Strip out of those clothes slowly." The corners of his mouth curved upward.

I did as he asked, and when I was completely naked, he held out his hand. Taking it, I climbed in between his legs and snuggled my back against him while his arm wrapped tightly around me.

"Ah. Those jets feels so good."

"Is that the only thing that feels good?" he asked as his hard cock pressed against my back.

Tilting my head back, I looked at him with a smile, and he lowered his until his lips met mine.

"How was your day?" he asked.

"Busy. Very busy. I need to hire a couple more people. How was your day?"

"Busy as usual. You know how much I love you, right?"

"What did you do?" I turned around and wrapped my legs around his waist.

"Why do you assume I did something? I just want you to hear that you know how much I love you."

I smiled at him as I ran my finger down his cheek. Then I poked him in the chest.

"What did you do, Sam?"

He let out a sigh. "I did nothing. With Stefan's situation, he's going to be in and out a lot while he figures out things with Lily. Therefore, I told Grayson today to work on getting me a personal assistant."

"Oh. Okay? That makes me happy. I know you need help. Frankly, I'm surprised you went this long without one. But why would you ask me if I knew how much you loved me?"

"Well…you know my track record. I just don't want you to feel insecure or anything."

"Do you really think I would? I know you love me, and I love you."

"I was just making sure because I don't want to do anything to upset you."

"You're the sweetest man in the world, Sam Kind, and you having a personal assistant wouldn't upset me, in the least."

"Good." He kissed my lips. "Because you know I'm not that man anymore. You've made me a better man, and I will spend the rest of my life thanking you for that, starting now." He grinned. "Get up here and let me show you how you're the only woman in the world for me."

～

"*H*ey, Josh." I looked at him in confusion because I hadn't seen him in a few days.

"Hey, Julia."

"Has Mrs. Bennett been on vacation or something? You haven't been in to get her coffee in a few days."

"No. Mrs. Bennett fired me. Hence the reason why I haven't been here."

"Oh no. Why did she fire you?"

"Because she's an evil self-absorbed bitch. That woman is the spawn of Satan. I was late because there was a bad accident on the 101. She texted me at five a.m. and told me she needed me to type up her notes for a seven a.m. meeting she was having downtown. A meeting she never told me about. So, I flew out of bed and got ready as fast as possible. But because of the accident, I couldn't get there in time to type up her notes and get them to her before her meeting. She told me I made her look like an unorganized idiot and that I was fired."

"Just because of that one incident?"

"Yes. I'd done everything for that woman over the past year. I should have known not to take the job when I found out nobody ever stays past six months. She's a miserable human being. Anyway, I'll take my usual mocha cream latte with an extra shot of espresso."

"I'm sorry, Josh."

"No biggie. I'll find another job. I'm just worried that no one will hire me since I got fired."

When I gave him his latte, he took it over to a table and pulled out his laptop.

Josh started coming into the café about a week after we opened. He came in every morning to get Mrs. Bennett's Americano on his way to work. We'd make small talk, and sometimes on his way home, he'd come in and get a coffee for himself. He always seemed stressed out and anxious, and I knew it stemmed from his job. He'd told me once that his boyfriend had broken up with him over it. He was such a sweet guy, and he didn't deserve to be treated the way he was. Then suddenly, it hit me. The universe was sending me a sign and slapping me right in the face with it.

I had called Grayson first thing this morning to see if he could meet with me today. I trusted my future husband. I really did. I knew how much he loved me, and he wouldn't do anything to jeopardize that. But I was a woman, and I just needed to speak to Grayson to lay down some rules about who could and couldn't work for Sam.

"Julia, your phone is ringing," Michelle said as she handed it to me.

"Hi, Grayson."

"Julia. It's good to hear from you. Sorry, it took me so long to return your call. I was in a meeting. "What's up?"

"Can you meet with me today?"

"Sure. What's this about?"

"I think you may already know."

"He told you?"

"Yes. And sitting in my coffee shop right now is a person whom I think would be perfect for Sam."

"Well, give me her number, and I'll give her a call to come in for an interview."

"We'll just come in now if you're available. Why wait? Right?"

"Um. Okay. I have an interview scheduled, but I can push it back."

"Thanks, Grayson. We'll see you soon. By the way, don't mention this to Sam."

"I won't."

After ending the call, I told Jasper that I had to leave for a while. After grabbing my purse, I walked over to where Josh sat and closed his laptop.

"Julia, what are you doing?"

"Grab your laptop and come with me. I'm taking you to a job interview."

"What? Where?"

"Kind Design & Architecture." I grinned. "Sam needs a personal assistant, and I think you're the perfect man for the job."

"Really?"

"Yeah. Come on. I'll give you all the job details on the way."

When we arrived at the office, I took the back way up to Grayson's office so I wouldn't run the risk of running into Sam. I'd asked Josh to wait outside Grayson's office while I talked to him first.

"Hi, Grayson." I smiled as I opened the door.

"Come in, Julia. Where's the candidate?"

"He's waiting outside your office."

"He?" His brow raised.

"Yes. He's perfect for the job. He used to work for a Mrs. Bennett."

"Quinn Bennett?"

"I guess."

"Oh, dear. She only hires male personal assistants because she likes to control them and makes their lives a living hell. I've heard that she does it because she couldn't control the other men in her life, aka, her three ex-husbands who cheated on her and left her for a younger woman. They don't last very long. Only a few months from what I hear."

"Josh was with her for a year."

"Send him in, and I'll interview him."

"No need to interview. He's perfect for Sam, and you'll hire him today." I grinned.

"Julia—"

"You'll hire him right now, Grayson. Then Sam will have his personal assistant, and I will be as happy as a clam."

He let out a long sigh as he leaned back in his chair and stared at me.

"He needs to fill out an application at least."

"That's fine."

I walked over to the door and opened it.

"Josh, you can come in now. This is Grayson. Grayson, meet Josh Handelman."

"It's nice to meet you, Josh." Grayson extended his hand.

"And you as well."

"Julia tells me you worked for Quinn Bennett?"

"I did."

"That must have been very challenging."

"To say the least."

"She's not a very nice woman," Grayson said.

"She's the spawn of Satan. I'm sorry. I shouldn't have said that."

"No. It's okay. She has quite a reputation."

Suddenly, the door opened, and Sam stuck his head in.

"I'm sorry, I didn't—Julia?" His brows furrowed. "What are you doing here?" He stepped inside.

*Crap.*

"Sam, I'd like you to meet your new personal assistant, Josh Handelman. Josh, this is Sam Kind. I'm sure you've seen him at the coffee shop."

"I have. It's a pleasure to meet you, Mr. Kind." Josh extended his hand.

"It's a pleasure to meet you too, Josh. I'm a little confused here."

"No need to be confused, Sam." I patted his chest. "He's your new personal assistant, and I need to use the restroom." I scurried out of Grayson's office, and he followed me.

"Julia Marie, stop right there!" I heard Sam's commanding voice.

I froze in place and slowly turned around. He walked over to me and cupped my chin with his hand.

"We'll talk about this tonight." A smirk crossed his lips. "I don't have time right now since I need to show my new personal assistant around."

"I drove him here, so I need to wait."

"Where's his car?"

"At the coffee shop. He just got fired from his last job, and he needs a new one. I immediately thought of you."

"Why would I want someone who got fired working for me?" His brow arched.

"He worked for Quinn Bennett." I chewed my bottom lip.

"Ouch. That woman is the worst possible human I know."

"Right? Now, don't you feel sorry for him?"

"I'll show him around, give him a couple of tasks and drive him back to the coffee shop later."

"You're the best future husband in the world!" I reached up and kissed his lips.

"As I said, we'll talk about this later." He walked away.

"I love you, Sam," I shouted.

"I love you, too." He turned his head with a smile on his face.

# CHAPTER 43

## TWO WEEKS LATER

Sam Julia and I stood on our bedroom terrace and watched Stefan and Lily build sandcastles on the beach.

"I can't believe the new nanny quit already. It's only been a week," Julia said.

"I think he hired her too soon. Lily isn't ready to accept someone else yet."

"Well, honestly, I didn't get a good vibe from that woman when I met her," she said.

"Me either. But Stefan was desperate. The problem is, I don't think Lily will ever accept anyone else."

"Has he thought about getting her some help? I think a good therapist can help her."

"He said he's not sending his kid to a shrink. I do think she has some issues, though. Between her mother abandoning her and Nanny Kate leaving."

"She's old enough to understand that Nanny Kate didn't have a choice," she said.

"I know. But it's still hard. It's going to take time, but I know she'll get through it." I reached over, placed my hand on hers, and gave it a gentle squeeze.

"I saw Josh at the coffee shop earlier today. He loves working for you, and he said he feels like he can breathe for the first time in over a year."

I let out a chuckle. "He's a great personal assistant. By the way, we never did talk about it that night."

"We didn't?" She glanced over at me.

"No. And you know we didn't. You used sex to avoid the conversation."

"I most certainly did not, Mr. Kind." She frowned.

"Yes. You did. When I came home, you were sprawled out on the bed wearing nothing but my favorite panties with candles burning and soft music playing."

"I missed you, and I wanted to do something special because you're an amazing man, and I love you."

"Uh-huh." I smirked.

"You don't believe me?"

"Admit it." I tapped her on the nose. "You were worried about who was going to work for me."

"Fine. Maybe one percent of me was. But the universe sent Josh to me to give to you." She grinned.

"Listen to me, Julia." I cupped her face in my hands. "I don't see any other women around me, even when I'm not with you. And do you know why?"

"Why?"

"Because I'm too busy loving you. You talk about the universe. Well, the universe sent you to me—the only woman I will ever look at and love with my whole heart." I brushed my lips against hers. "We need to set a date for the wedding right now. You keep calling me your future husband, and as much as I love to hear it, I don't want to be your future husband for much longer. I want to be your husband, and I want you to be my wife."

The corners of her mouth curved upward as she softly kissed me.

"Let's look at venues tomorrow and find the soonest date we can."

"I already called The Beverly Hills Hotel. We can have a garden ceremony like my father did and have the reception in the ballroom. They had a cancellation for June 1st, and I put down a deposit."

"That's in three months, Sam."

"I know. I think it's perfect, don't you?"

"It's a perfect date, but three months isn't enough time to plan the perfect wedding. I may need to steal your personal assistant for some help."

"You have your sister and your mom. Why do you need Josh?"

"Why are you questioning me, Sam?" Her brow raised.

"Right. He's all yours if you need him."

"Thank you." Her lips gave way to a gorgeous smile, and she began to walk away. Grabbing her hand, I pulled her back to me.

"Where do you think you're going?"

"To call my parents and Jenni to tell them we've set a date."

"I don't think so." I led her over to the bed. "We have some wedding date celebrating to do first." I grinned as I pushed her on the bed and climbed on top of her.

~

*N*ow that Julia and I had set a wedding date, it was time to put the plans in motion. For as many times as I stood up at my father's weddings, I never once saw myself being the groom and waiting for my bride to walk down the aisle to me. I only saw myself as a bachelor and living the best life I could with my brothers until a beautiful woman gave me the last apple turnover one morning at the Starlight Café.

Julia Benton blew into my life like a hurricane, and without warning. I'd broken the pact my brothers and I made all those years ago. Someone had to be the first, and now I could only hope after seeing how much Julia and I loved each other, they would find the courage to find a love of their own.

Thank you for reading One of a Kind! I hope you enjoyed Sam & Julia's story.

Are you interested in a BONUS CHAPTER? Click the link below!

Bonus Chapter

*W*ill Stefan find a new nanny to stick around for his nine-year-old daughter, Lily? Will he ever allow himself to find love like his brother Sam? Find out in the next installment of the Kind Brothers Series: Two of a Kind.

Download Here

*I*'d like to invite you to join my Sandi's Romance Readers Facebook Group where we talk about books, romance and more! Come join the fun!

*Y*ou can also join my romance tribe by following me on social media and subscribing to my newsletter to keep up with my new releases, sales, cover reveals and more!

Newsletter
Website
Facebook
Instagram
Bookbub
Goodreads

Looking for more romance reads about billionaires, second chances and sports? Check out my other romance novels and escape to another world and from the daily grind of life – one book at a time.

Series:

*Forever Series*
Forever Black (Forever, Book 1)
Forever You (Forever, Book 2)
Forever Us (Forever, Book 3)

Being Julia (Forever, Book 4)
Collin (Forever, Book 5)
A Forever Family (Forever, Book 6)
A Forever Christmas (Holiday short story)

*Wyatt Brothers*
Love, Lust & A Millionaire (Wyatt Brothers, Book 1)
Love, Lust & Liam (Wyatt Brothers, Book 2)

*A Millionaire's Love*
Lie Next to Me (A Millionaire's Love, Book 1)
When I Lie with You (A Millionaire's Love, Book 2)

*Happened Series*
Then You Happened (Happened Series, Book 1)
Then We Happened (Happened Series, Book 2)

*Redemption Series*
Carter Grayson (Redemption Series, Book 1)
Chase Calloway (Redemption Series, Book 2)
Jamieson Finn (Redemption Series, Book 3)
Damien Prescott (Redemption Series, Book 4)

*Interview Series*

The Interview: New York & Los Angeles Part 1
The Interview: New York & Los Angeles Part 2

*Love Series:*
Love In Between (Love Series, Book 1)
The Upside of Love (Love Series, Book 2)

*Wolfe Brothers*
Elijah Wolfe (Wolfe Brothers, Book 1)
Nathan Wolfe (Wolfe Brothers, Book 2)
Mason Wolfe (Wolfe Brothers, Book 3)

*Kind Brothers*
One of a Kind (Kind Brothers, Book 1)
Two of a Kind (Kind Brothers, Book 2)
Three of a Kind (Kind Brothers, Book 3)
Four of a Kind (Kind Brothers, Book 4)
Five of a Kind (Kind Brothers, Book 5)
The Kind Brothers (Kind Brothers, Book 6)

*Standalone Books*

The Billionaire's Christmas Baby
His Proposed Deal
The Secret He Holds
The Seduction of Alex Parker
Something About Lorelei
One Night in London